# BOOKS

## Venus Drive
### Stories by Sam Lipsyte

"Sam Lipsyte is a wickedly gifted writer. *Venus Drive* is filled with grimly satisfying fractured insights and hardcore humor. But it also displays some inspired sympathy for the daze and confusion of its characters. Above all it's wonderfully written and compulsively readable with brilliant and funny dialogue, a collection that represents the emergence of a very strong talent."
  —Robert Stone

"Sam Lipsyte can get blood out of a stone—rich, red human blood from the stony sterility of contemporary life. His writing is gripping—at least I gripped this book so hard my knuckles turned white."
  —Edmund White

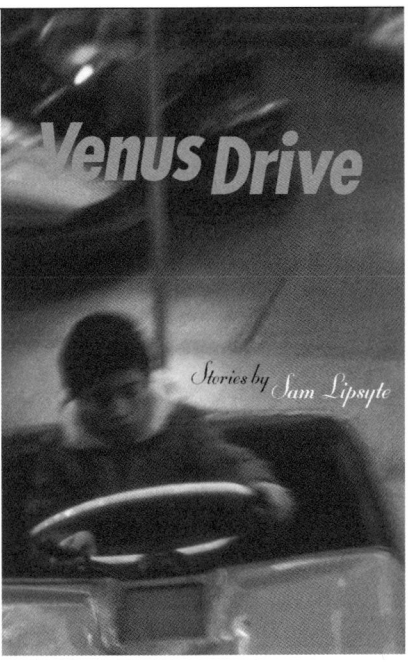

## Karoo
### A Novel by Steve Tesich

"Fascinating—a real satiric invention full of wise outrage."
  —Arthur Miller

"A powerful and deeply disturbing portrait of a flawed, self-destructive, and compulsively fascinating figure."
  —*Kirkus Reviews* (starred)

"Saul Karoo is a new kind of wild man, the sane maniac. Larger than life and all too human, his out-of-control odyssey through sex, death, and show business is extreme, and so is the pleasure of reading it. Steve Tesich created a fabulously Gargantuan comic character."
  —Michael Herr

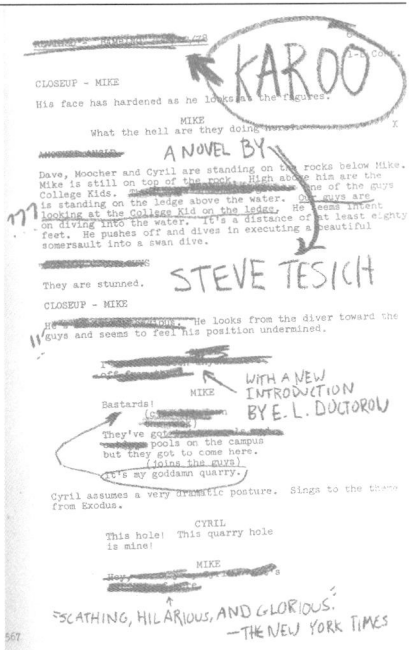

 **OPEN CITY**

## Some Hope
### A Trilogy by Edward St. Aubyn

"Tantalizing . . . A memorable tour de force."
  —*The New York Times Book Review*

"Hilarious and harrowing by turns, sophisticated, reflective, and brooding."
  —*The New York Review of Books*

"Feverishly good writing . . . Full of Algonquin wit on the surface while roiling underneath. *Some Hope* is a hell of a brew, as crisp and dry as a good English cider and as worth savoring as any of Waugh's most savage volleys."
  —*The Ruminator Review*

## Mother's Milk
### A Novel by Edward St. Aubyn

"St. Aubyn's caustic, splendid novel probes the slow violence of blood ties—a superbly realized agenda hinted at in the novel's arresting first sentence: 'Why had they pretended to kill him when he was born?'"
  —*The Village Voice*

"Postpartum depression, assisted suicide, adultery, alcoholism—it's all here in St. Aubyn's keenly observed, perversely funny novel about an illustrious cosmopolitan family and the mercurial matriarch who rules them all."
  —*People*

# OPEN CITY

New York City, Winter 2010
Number Twenty-Eight

 **OPEN CITY**

# Actual Air
## Poems by David Berman

"David Berman's poems are beautiful, strange, intelligent, and funny. They are narratives that freeze life in impossible contortions. They take the familiar and make it new, so new the reader is stunned and will not soon forget. I found much to savor on every page of *Actual Air*. It's a book for everyone."
—James Tate

"This is the voice I have been waiting so long to hear . . . Any reader who tunes in to his snappy, offbeat meditations is in for a steady infusion of surprises and delights."
—Billy Collins

# My Misspent Youth
## Essays by Meghan Daum

"An empathic reporter and a provocative autobiographer . . . I finished it in a single afternoon, mesmerized and sputtering."
—*The Nation*

"Meghan Daum articulates the only secret left in the culture: discreet but powerful fantasies of romance, elegance, and ease that survive in our uncomfortable world of striving. These essays are very smart and very witty and just heartbreaking enough to be deeply pleasurable."
—Marcelle Clements

# BOOKS

## Goodbye, Goodness
### A Novel by Sam Brumbaugh

"*Goodbye, Goodness* is the rock n' roll
*Great Gatsby*."
—New City Chicago

"Sam Brumbaugh's debut novel couldn't
be more timely. *Goodbye, Goodness*
boasts just enough sea air and action to
make an appealing summer read without coming anywhere near fluffsville."
—*Time Out New York*

"Beautifully captures the wrung-out feel
of a depleted American century."
—*Baltimore City Paper*

## The First Hurt
### Stories by Rachel Sherman

"Sherman's writing is sharp, hard, and
honest; there's a fearlessness in her
work, an I'm-not-afraid-to-say-this quality.
Because she knows that most of us
have thought the same but didn't have
the guts to say it."
—*Boston Phoenix*

"Rachel Sherman writes stories like splinters: they get under your skin and stay
with you long after you've closed the
book. These haunting stories are both
wonderfully, deeply weird and unset-
tlingly familiar."
—Judy Budnitz

# OPEN CITY

## Long Live a Hunger to Feed Each Other
### Poems by Jerome Badanes

"Reading Jerome Badanes's poems is not so much reading a voice from the heartfelt past as reading a poet whose work is very much alive and yet reflects a lost—and meaningful—age. He is one of our good souls; he is one of our poets. I treasure his work."
   —Gerald Stern

"The best best book publishing story of the year."
   —Poetry

## Farewell Navigator
### Stories by Leni Zumas

"Zumas gives socially awkward, mysteriously gifted and self-destructive outcasts spellbinding, unflinching voice. . . . It's a powerful, irresistible collection."
   —Publishers Weekly

"Leni Zumas's writing is fearless and swift, sassy and sensational."
   —Joy Williams

"I have never read stories like these before and I can't get them out of my head. Her language is real sorcery—it dismantles the world you think you know and takes you to strange, fecund territories of the imagination. "
   —Karen Russell

# BOOKS

## Love Without
### Stories by Jerry Stahl

"[Stahl]...knows how to shock us into
laughter, and his best work mines the
grotesque for pathos, a tradition that
includes Flannery O'Connor, Barry
Hannah, and Denis Johnson . . .The key
isn't whom he writes about, but at what
depth . . . Stahl plunges us into depraved
worlds with a keen intensity of purpose,
and his addled protagonists run up hard
against the truth of their desires."
　　—Los Angeles Times

"Tender and gut-busting."
　　—L.A. Weekly

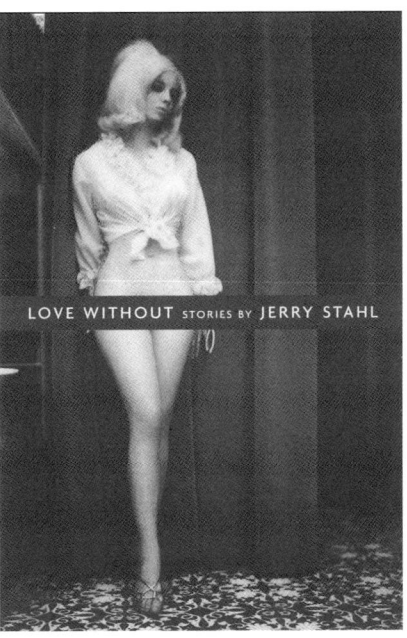

## Why the Devil Chose New England for His Work
### Stories by Jason Brown

"Links gem-cut stories of troubled
youths, alcoholics, illicit romances, the
burden of inheritance, and the bane of
class, all set in the dense upper reaches
of Maine, and delivers them with hope,
heart, and quiet humor."
　　—Elle

"The inhabitants of Vaughn, Maine are
stalked not by Stephen King horror but
by intimate afflictions of blood, accident,
and history, heart, and quiet humor."
　　—The Boston Globe

# OPEN CITY BOOKS

## Flight Patterns
### A Century of Stories about Flying
### Edited by Dorothy Spears

This anthology of stories about air travel features writing by: Orville Wright, Charles A. Lindbergh, James Salter, Mary Gaitskill, Tobias Wolff, Grace Paley, Walter Kirn, Alice Munro, Jerry Stahl, Antione de Saint Exupèry, Thomas Beller, Tom Wolfe, Joseph Heller, James Dickey, Erica Jong, Saïd Sayrafiezadeh, Roald Dahl, Meghan Daum, Barry Hannah, Beryl Markham, Mary Lee Settle, Amelia Earhart, Sheila M. Schwartz, Manuel Gonzales, Jonathan Tel, Rachel Cantor, Bernard Chabbert, John Bowe, Gary Horn, Brad Kessler, and Linda Yablonsky.

## Living Room
### A Novel by Rachel Sherman

"A compelling and unsentimental novel about the loneliness that exists just below the surface of a family. Sherman skillfully and movingly renders the inner lives of three generations of women as they try—or don't try—to reconcile the distance between their desires and their actual lives."
   —Dana Spiotta

"A riveting debut novel...Unsentimental yet deeply felt, this tale examines what bubbles under the surface of a supposedly happy Long Island family."
   —Publishers Weekly (starred review)

# OPEN CITY

# OPEN CITY

*Open City* is published by Open City, Inc., a nonprofit corporation. Donations are tax-deductible to the extent allowed by the law. A one-year subscription (3 issues) is $30; a two-year subscription (6 issues) is $55. Make checks payable to: Open City, Inc., 270 Lafayette Street, Suite 1412, New York, NY 10012. For credit-card orders, see our Web site: www.opencity.org. E-mail: editors@opencity.org.

Open City is a member of the Council of Literary Magazines and Presses and is indexed by Humanities International Complete.

Open City gratefully acknowledges the generous support of the family of Robert Bingham. We also thank the New York State Council on the Arts, a state agency. See the page following the masthead for additional donor acknowledgments.

Front and back covers by Miranda Lichtenstein.
Front: *Untitled #55*, 2009, chromogenic print. Back: *Untitled #17*, 2009, chromogenic print. Courtesy of the artist and Elizabeth Dee Gallery.

Front page drawing by Joseph Ayers. *Raft of the Medusa*, 2008, graphite on paper. Courtesy of Franklin Parrasch Gallery.

ISBN-13: 978-1-890447-54-0
ISBN-10: 1-890447-54-4
ISSN: 1089-5523

# OPEN CITY

**EDITORS**
Thomas Beller
Joanna Yas

**ART DIRECTOR**
Nick Stone

**EDITOR-AT-LARGE**
Adrian Dannatt

**CONTRIBUTING EDITORS**

Alex Abramovich
Jonathan Ames
Elizabeth Beller
David Berman
Aimée Bianca
Will Blythe
Jason Brown
Sam Brumbaugh
Patrick Gallagher
Amanda Gersh
Laura Hoffmann
Jan de Jong
Kip Kotzen
Anthony Lacavaro

Vanessa Lilly
Sam Lipsyte
Jim Merlis
Honor Moore
Parker Posey
Beatrice von Rezzori
Elizabeth Schmidt
Lee Smith
Dorothy Spears
Maxine Swann
Alexandra Tager
Tony Torn
Jocko Weyland
Edmund White

**DEVELOPMENT DIRECTOR**
Kimberly King Parsons

**INTERNS**
Nick Earhart
Lina Makdisi

**READERS**
Mike Gardner
Michael Hornburg
Sarah LaPolla
Rowland Miller
Ana Saldamando

**FOUNDING EDITORS**
Thomas Beller
Daniel Pinchbeck

**FOUNDING PUBLISHER**
Robert Bingham

OPEN CITY WOULD LIKE TO THANK

THE FOLLOWING FOR THEIR GENEROUS CONTRIBUTIONS

### Patrons ($1,000 or more)
Hava Beller
Clara Bingham
Joan Bingham
Belle & Henry Davis
Lee Flanagan
Wendy Flanagan
Laura Fontana & John J. Moore
Alex Kuczynski
Vanessa & John Lilly
Gary Lippman
Eleanor & Rowland Miller
Richard Serra
Scott Smith
Dorothy Spears

### Donors ($500 or more)
Jonathan Ames
Adelaide De Menil
Laura Fontana
Amy & Bill Frischling
Richard Makdisi
David Selig (Rice Restaurant)
Ben Stiller & Christine Taylor

### Contributors ($150 or more)

R. Scott Asen
Molly Bingham
Duncan Birmingham
Sara Burns
Sarah Borden
Patricia Bosworth
Toby Bryce
Nina Collins
Joe Conason & Elizabeth Wagley
Holly Dando
Tiffany & Justin Foa
Edward Garmey
David Goodwillie
Pierre Hauser
Carol Irving
Kathy Kemp

Ann Marlowe
William Morton
Jason Kliot & Joana Vicente
Caitlin Macy & Jeremy Barnum
Rulonna Neilson
Tim Nye
Jonathan Rabinowitz
Rick Rofihe
Jennifer & Ben Ruff
Robert Soros &
	Melissa Schiff Soros
Jennifer Sturman
Judson Traphagan
Shelley Wanger
Chris Young

# Friends

Henry Alcalay
Alex Abramovich
Lucy Anderson
Tony Antoniadis
Harold Augenbraum
Noah Baumbach
Alex Baxter
Madeleine Beckman
Madison Smartt Bell
Elizabeth Beller
Betsy Berne
Aimée Bianca
Andrew Blauner
Paula Bomer
Ghurron Briscoe
Sam Brumbaugh
Jocelyn Casey-Whitman
Simon Constable
Paula Cooper
Thomas Cregan
Adrian Dannatt
John Donahue
Christopher Edgar
Erin Edmison
Deborah Eisenberg
Lisa Evanchuck
Mary Evans
Jofie Ferrari-Adler
Mike Gardner
Deborah Garrison
Alice Gordon
Melissa Gould
Melissa Grace
Rebecca Green
Will Heinrich
Laura Hoffmann
Jessamyn Hope
Gerald Howard
Amy Hundley

Anthony Lacavaro
Deborah Landau
Matt Lee
Guy Lesser
Sam Lipsyte
Stephen Mark
Pearson Marx
Vestal McIntyre
Paul Morris
Carolyn Murnick
Christopher Nicholson
Ethan Nosowsky
Nancy Novogrod
Sylvia Paret
Vince Passaro
Francine Prose
Beatrice von Rezzori
Anne Rivers
Saïd Sayrafiezadeh
Elizabeth Schmidt
Richard Serra
Wallace Shawn
Rachel Sherman
Claudia Silver
Debra Singer
Betsy Smith
Lee Smith
Valerie Steiker
Anna Stein
Nick Stone
Robert Stone
Stefanie Syman
Paul Tullis
Ben Turner
Dean Wareham & Britta Phillips
Cecilia & John Weyland
Malerie Willens
Leni Zumas
Todd Zuniga

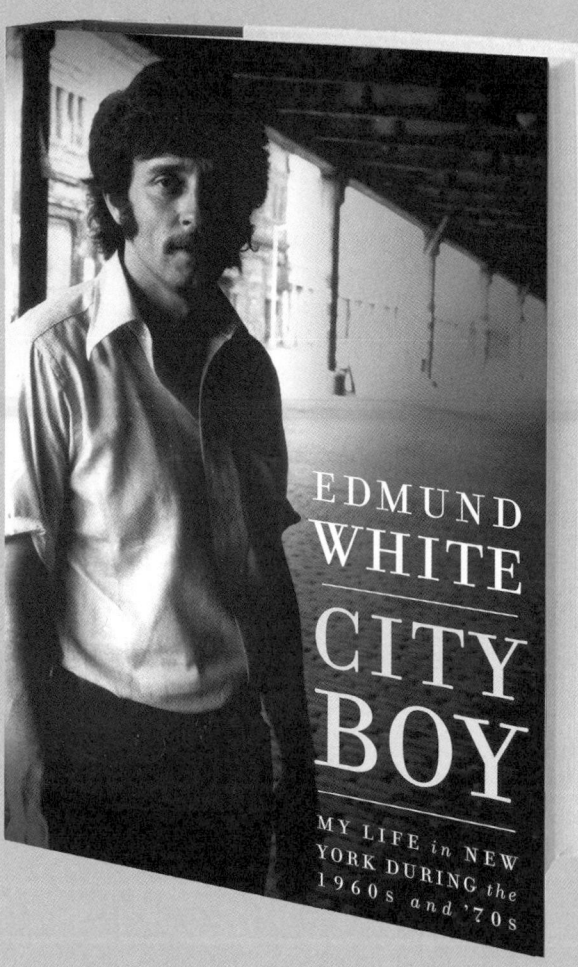

# ANNA

CLOTHES FOR WOMEN

150 East 3rd Street at Avenue A
New York City
212.358.0195
www.annanyc.com

# ACADEMY AWARD® NOMINEE

"Forceful and important...gripping."
–The New York Times

## The
# RESTLESSCONSCIENCE
## RESISTANCE TO HITLER IN NAZI GERMANY
A Film by Hava Kohav Beller

"Graceful...Devastating...
It's a provocative examination of ethics put to the gravest test imaginable."
– The Wall Street Journal

# AVAILABLE NOW
## ON DVD, ITUNES, AND NETFLIX

" . . .Very moving documentary . . . fascinating . . . intense and powerful."
—**Georgia Brown,** *The Village Voice*

"Hava Kohav Beller's remarkable, Oscar-nominated documentary about anti-Nazi resistance in Germany between 1933 and 1945 is a heartbreaking historical work . . . Fictional accounts pale by comparison."
—**Hal Hinson,** *The Washington Post*

" . . . A compelling work of historical and human significance."
—**John Kenneth Galbraith**

"The film has passion and depth that is rare in documentaries today."
—**Richard Hutton, WNET/Thirteen**

"Tough, impassioned document . . . vivid, heartbreaking . . . powerful and important."
—**Edward Guthmann,** *San Francisco Chronicle*

"Devastating . . . deeply affecting . . . unique."
—**David Armstrong,** *San Francisco Examiner*

"Hava Kohav Beller's gripping documentary . . . is a powerful piece of work."
—**Harry Haun,** *The Daily News*

"A fresh moral perspective on Nazism's trajectory . . . The film's value can scarcely be overstated . . . Searing and unforgettable power."
—**Godfrey Cheshire,** *New York Press*

**www.therestlessconscience.com**

anderbo.com "Best New Online Journal"
—storySouth Million Writers Award

# anderbo.com

fiction    poetry    "fact"    photography

# RROFIHE TROPHY!

## 2009 WINNER
## LESLIE MASLOW

### FOR HER STORY
### "MUM"

There were 244 stories submitted to the
2009 RRofihe Trophy Contest.

Leslie Maslow's story
is published in this issue.
She also receives $500 and a trophy.

### 2010 RRofihe Trophy Guidelines

- Stories should be typed, double-spaced, on 8 1/2 x 11 paper with the author's name and contact information on the first page and name and story title on the upper right corner of remaining pages
- Submissions must be postmarked by October 15, 2010
- Limit one submission per author
- Author must not have been previously published in *Open City*
- Mail submissions to RRofihe, 270 Lafayette Street, Suite 1412, New York, NY 10012
- Enclose self-addressed stamped business envelope to receive names of winner and honorable mentions
- All manuscripts are non-returnable and will be recycled
- Reading fee is $10. Check or money order payable to RRofihe
- Judged by Rick Rofihe; 2010 Contest Assistant: Carolyn Wilsey

"Theroux speaks honestly about the quotidian and miraculous aspects of loss and new chances. It's all here—births, deaths, and marriages—and the reader is invited into the intimacies of a world that is both familiar and full of surprises."

—ELIZABETH STROUT, AUTHOR OF *OLIVE KITTERIDGE*

"I loved this singularly honest and graceful book. Phyllis Theroux reminds us that there is no such thing as an ordinary moment, and certainly no such thing as an ordinary

—ELIZABETH GILBERT, best-selling author of *Eat, Pray, Love*

THE
JOURNAL KEEPER
*A Memoir*

PHYLLIS THEROUX

"I loved this singularly honest and graceful book. *The Journal Keeper* reminds us that there is no such thing as an ordinary moment, and certainly no such thing as an ordinary life."—ELIZABETH GILBERT, AUTHOR OF *EAT, PRAY, LOVE*

ATLANTIC MONTHLY PRESS
an imprint of Grove/Atlantic, Inc.
Distributed by Publishers Group West

forthcoming in March 2010
www.writers-well.com

# LOST AND FOUND

## STORIES FROM NEW YORK, VOL. II

### EDITED BY
### THOMAS BELLER

Essays from Mr. Beller's Neighborhood by:

Charles D'Ambrosio, Rachel Cline, Meghan Daum, Hal Sirowitz, Matthew Roberts, Debbie Nathan, Saïd Sayrafiezadeh, Rachel Sherman, Bryan Charles, Phillip Lopate, Jonathan Ames, Alicia Erian, Madison Smartt Bell, Betsy Berne, Thomas Beller, Sam Lipsyte, and more.

Spring 2009
Mr. Beller's Neighborhood Books
Distributed by W.W. Norton

www.mrbellersneighborhood.com

# CONTRIBUTORS' NOTES

**SOPHIE CABOT BLACK** has two poetry collections, *The Misunderstanding of Nature*, which received the Poetry Society of America's First Book Award and *The Descent*, which received the 2005 Connecticut Book Award. Her poetry has appeared in numerous magazines, including *The Atlantic Monthly*, *The New Republic*, *The New Yorker*, and *The Paris Review*. She currently teaches at Columbia University.

**JONATHAN DEE** is the author of five novels, including the forthcoming *The Privileges*, from which his piece in this issue is excerpted. He is a staff writer for *The New York Times Magazine*, a frequent contributor to *Harper's*, and a former senior editor of *The Paris Review*. He teaches in the graduate writing programs at Columbia University and the New School.

**LOUIS B. JONES** has published three novels: *Ordinary Money*, *Particles and Luck*, and *California's Over*, all named *New York Times* Notable Books. He is an NEA fellow and a fellow of the MacDowell Colony. He has written screenplays—originals and adaptations of his own work—for studios and for independents. For some years he has been fiction director for the Squaw Valley Community of Writers.

**GARY LIPPMAN** is a lawyer (currently doing part-time pro bono work at New York's Innocence Project), and a father, not necessarily in that order. His play *Paradox Lust* was produced off-Broadway in 2001, and six of his *Stories for People with a Modern Attention Span* appeared in *Open City* 28. His piece in this issue is excerpted from his as-yet-unpublished novel *We Loved the World But Could Not Stay*.

**SAM LIPSYTE** is the author of the story collection *Venus Drive*, and the novels *The Subject Steve* and *Home Land*. His contribution to this issue is an excerpt from his forthcoming novel, *The Ask*. He lives in New York City and teaches creative writing at Columbia University.

**MIRANDA LICHTENSTEIN** (cover) is represented by Elizabeth Dee in New York and Gallery Min Min in Tokyo. She was a recent fellow at the Civitella Ranieri Center in Umbertide, Italy. She lives and works in New York City.

**SARAH MALONE** is in the MFA program in fiction at the University of Massachusetts Amherst and blogs about things literary and otherwise at sarahwrotethat.com. This is her first published story.

**LESLIE MASLOW** grew up in Wilkes-Barre, Pennsylvania and now lives in Brooklyn. She attended Oberlin and received an MFA in playwriting from the New School in 1999. This is her first published story.

**MICHAEL McGRATH** is currently a Hoyns/Poe-Faulkner Fellow at the University of Virginia, where he reads, writes, and teaches. This is his first published story.

**BEN NACHUMI** is an underemployed physicist and tutor living in Brooklyn. This is his second appearance in *Open City*.

**KEVIN OBERLIN** lives and writes in Cincinnati. He holds an MFA from the University of Maryland, College Park, and his chapbook *Spotlit Girl* won the 2007 Wick Poetry Center Chapbook Prize.

**ADAM PETERSON** lives in Houston, Texas, where he is the co-editor of *The Cupboard*. His work has recently appeared or is forthcoming in *Alaska Quarterly Review*, *Cincinnati Review*, and *Denver Quarterly* among other journals.

**JAMES SCHUYLER** (1923–1991) received the Pulitzer Prize in poetry for *The Morning of the Poem* in 1981. The poems in this issue are forthcoming in *Other Flowers: Uncollected Poems*, edited by James Meetze and Simon Pettet.

**DAN SOFAER** graduated from the University of Chicago, and also studied classics in Hebrew at the Hebrew University of Jerusalem. He took classes as an adult student in drawing and painting at the Ecole des Beaux Arts in Paris. He then studied more Greek and Latin at UC Berkeley where he wrote an article on Aristophanes' songs in *The Birds*. He lives in Woodstock, New York, and Yelping Hill, Connecticut.

**CHRISTOPHER SORRENTINO** has written three books, including *Trance*, a National Book Award finalist. He is currently working on a novel about identity.

**LAURIE STONE** is author of three books of fiction and nonfiction and has published memoir pieces in *Creative Nonfiction*, *TriQuarterly*, and *Threepenny Review*, among other publications. A longtime writer for *The Village Voice*, *The Nation*, and *Ms. Magazine*, she is currently at work on *My Life As an Animal: A Memoir in Stories*, *Unmarked Trail: A Romance in Stories*, and a guide to setting up a writing partnership in collaboration with Richard Toon.

# NICK STONE DESIGN

50 Pine Street #5S New York, NY 10005

stone@nickstonedesign.com

www.nickstonedesign.com

T: 212.995.1863

F: 212.353.0592

M: 718.791.3960

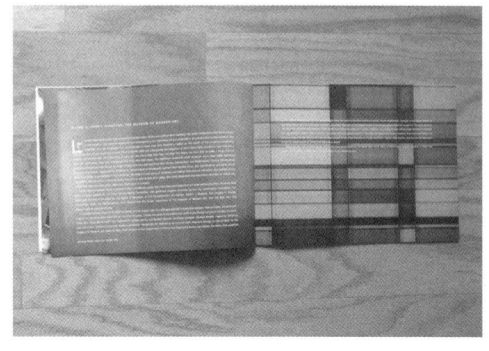

# LINCOLN PLAZA CINEMAS

Six Screens

63RD STREET & BROADWAY
OPPOSITE LINCOLN CENTER
212-757-2280

# OPEN

"The Crazy Person" by Mary Gaitskill, "La Vie en Rose" by Hubert Selby Jr., "Cathedral Parkway" by Vince Passaro. Art by Jeff Koons and Devon Dikeou. Cover by Ken Schles, whose *Invisible City* sells for thousands on Ebay. Stan Friedman's poems about baldness and astronomy, Robert Polito on Lester Bangs, Jon Tower's real life letters to astronauts. (Vastly underpriced at $500. Only two copies left.)

A first glimpse of Martha McPhee; a late burst from Terry Southern. Jaime Manrique's "Twilight at the Equator." Art by Paul Ramirez-Jonas, Kate Milford, Richard Serra. Kip Kotzen's "Skate Dogs," Richard Foreman's "Poetry City" with playful illustrations by Daniel Pinchbeck, David Shields' "Sports" and his own brutal youth. (Ken Schles found the negative of our cover girl on Thirteenth Street and Avenue B. We're still looking for the girl. $25)

Irvine Welsh's "Eurotrash" (his American debut), Richard Yates (from his last, unfinished novel), Patrick McCabe (years before *The Butcher Boy*). Art by Francesca Woodman (with an essay by Betsy Berne), Jacqueline Humphries, Allen Ginsberg, Alix Lambert. A short shot of Lipsyte—"Shed"—not available anywhere else. Plus Alfred Chester's letters to Paul Bowles. Chip Kidd riffs on the Fab Four. (Very few copies left! $100)

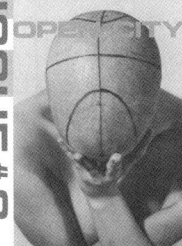

Stories by the always cheerful Cyril Connolly ("Happy Deathbeds"), Thomas McGuane, Jim Thompson, Samantha Gillison, Michael Brownstein, and Emily Carter, whose "Glory Goes and Gets Some" was reprinted in *Best American Short Stories.* Art by Julianne Swartz and Peter Nadin. Poems by David Berman and Nick Tosches. Plus Denis Johnson in Somalia. (A monster issue, sales undercut by slightly rash choice of cover art by editors. Get it while you can! $15)

*Change or Die*
Stories by David Foster Wallace, Siobhan Reagan, Irvine Welsh. Jerome Badanes' brilliant novella, "Change or Die" (film rights still available). Poems by David Berman and Vito Acconci. Plus Helen Thorpe on the murder of Ireland's most famous female journalist, and Delmore Schwartz on T. S. Eliot's squint. (Still sold-out! Wait for e-books to catch on or band together and demand a reprint.)

# CITY back issues

*Make an investment in your future…*
In today's volatile marketplace
you could do worse.

### The Only Woman He's Ever Left
Stories by James Purdy, Jocko Weyland, Strawberry Saroyan. Michael Cunningham's "The Slap of Love." Poems by Rick Moody, Deborah Garrison, Monica Lewinsky, Charlie Smith. Art by Matthew Ritchie, Ellen Harvey, Cindy Stefans. Rem Koolhaas project. With a beautiful cover by Adam Fuss. (Only $10 for this blockbuster.)

### The Rubbed Away Girl
Stories by Mary Gaitskill, Bliss Broyard, and Sam Lipsyte. Art by Jimmy Raskin, Laura Larson, and Jeff Burton. Poems by David Berman, Elizabeth Macklin, Stephen Malkmus, and Will Oldham. (We found some copies in the back of the closet so were able to lower the price! $25 (it *was* $50))

### Beautiful to Strangers
Stories by Caitlin O'Connor Creevy, Joyce Johnson, and Amine Wefali, back when her byline was Zaitzeff (now the name of her organic sandwich store at Nassau & John Streets—go there for lunch!). Poems by Harvey Shapiro, Jeffrey Skinner, and Daniil Kharms. Art by David Robbins, Liam Gillick, and Elliott Puckette. Piotr Uklanski's cover is a panoramic view of Queens, shot from the top of the World Trade Center in 1998. ($10)

### Bewitched
Stories by Jonathan Ames, Said Shirazi, and Sam Lipsyte. Essays by Geoff Dyer and Alexander Chancellor, who hates rabbit. Poems by Chan Marshall, Lucy Anderson, and Edvard Munch on intimate and sensitive subjects. Art by Karen Kilimnick, Giuseppe Penone, Mark Leckey, Maurizio Cattelan, and M.I.M.E. (Our bestselling issue. ($10))

### Editors' Issue
Previously demure editors publish themselves. Enormous changes at the last minute. Stories by Robert Bingham, Thomas Beller, Daniel Pinchbeck, Joanna Yas, Adrian Dannatt, Kip Kotzen, Geoffrey O' Brien, Lee Smith, Amanda Gersh, and Jocko Weyland. Poems by Tony Torn. Art by Nick Stone, Meghan Gerety, and Alix Lambert. (Years later, Ken Schles's cover photo appears on a Richard Price novel.) ($10)

ISSUE #6

ISSUE #7

ISSUE #8

ISSUE #9

ISSUE #10

# OPEN

*Octo Ate Them All*

Vestal McIntyre emerges from the slush pile like aphrodite with a brilliant story that corresponds to the tattoo that covers his entire back. Siobhan Reagan thinks about strangulation. Fiction by Melissa Pritchard and Bill Broun. Anthropologist Michael Taussig's Cocaine Museum. Gregor von Rezzori's meditation on solitude, sex, and raw meat. Art by Joanna Kirk, Sebastien de Ganay, and Ena Swansea. ($10)

ISSUE # 11

OPEN CITY

*Equivocal Landscape*

Sam Brumbaugh, author of *Goodbye, Goodness*, debuts with a story set in Kenya, Daphne Beal and Swamiji, Paula Bomer sees red on a plane, Heather Larimer hits a dog, and Hunter Kennedy on the sexual possibilities of Charlottesville versus West Texas. Ford Madox Ford on the end of fun. Poetry by Jill Bialosky and Rachel Wetzsteon. Art by Miranda Lichtenstein and Pieter Schoolwerth; a love scene by Toru Hayashi. Mungo Thomson passes notes. ($10)

ISSUE # 12

OPEN CITY

*Hi-fi*

Sam Lipsyte introduces Steve. Nick Tosches smokes with God. Jack Walls remembers the gangs of Chicago. Vince Passaro ponders adult content. Poetry by Honor Moore, Sarah Gorham, and Melissa Holbrook Pierson. Mini-screenplay by Terry Southern. Art by Luisa Kazanas, Peter Pinchbeck, and Julianne Swartz. Special playwrighting section guest edited by Tony Torn. ($10)

ISSUE # 13

OPEN CITY

*Something Like Ten Million*

The defacto life and death issue. Amazing debut stories from Nico Baumbach, Michiko Okubo, and Sarah Porter; Craig Chester writes on why he has the face he deserves; a bushy, funny, and phallic art project from Louise Belcourt. Special poetry section guest edited by Lee Ann Brown. A photo essay of fleeing Manhattanites by Ken Schles. The cover is beautiful and weird, a bright hole in downtown Manhattan. ($10)

ISSUE # 14

OPEN CITY

*That Russian Question*

Another excerpt from Amine Wefali's *Westchester Burning (see Open City #8)*. Alicia Erian in *Jeopardy*. Jocko Weyland does handplants for an audience of elk. James Lasdun on travel and infidelity. Lara Vapnyar's debut publication. Poetry by Steve Healy, Daniel Nester, Lev Rubinshtein, and Daniel Greene. ($10)

ISSUE # 15

OPEN CITY

# CITY

Please send a check or
money order payable to:

Open City, Inc.
270 Lafayette Street, Suite 1412
New York, NY 10012

For credit-card orders, see www.opencity.org.

*I wait, I wait.*
A brilliant outtake from Robert Bingham's *Lightning on the Sun*. Ryan Kenealy on the girl who ran off with the circus; Nick Tosches on Proust. Art by Allen Ruppersberg, David Bunn, Nina Katchadourian, Matthew Higgs, and Matthew Brannon. Stories by Evan Harris, Lewis Robinson, Michael Sledge, and Bruce Jay Friedman. Rick Rofihe feels Marlene. Poetry by Dana Goodyear, Nathaniel Bellows, and Kevin Young. ($10)

*They're at it again.*
Lara Vapnyar's "There Are Jews in My House," Chuck Kinder on Dagmar. Special poetry section guest edited by Honor Moore, including C. K. Williams, Victoria Redel, Eamon Grennan, and Carolyn Forché. Art by Stu Mead, Christoph Heemann, Jason Fox, Herzog film star Bruno S., and Sophie Toulouse, whose "Sexy Clowns" project has become a "character note for [our] intentions" (says the *Literary Magazine Review*). See what all the fuss is about. ($10)

*I Want to Be Your Shoebox*
Susan Chamandy on Hannibal's elephants and hockey, Mike Newirth's noirish "Semiprecious." Rachel Blake's "Elephants" (an unintentional elephant theme emerges). Poetry by Catherine Bowman and Rodney Jack. Art by Viggo Mortensen, Alix Lambert, Marcellus Hall, Mark Solotroff, and Alaskan Pipeline polar bear cover by Jason Middlebrook (we're still trying to figure out what the bear had for lunch). ($10)

*Post Hoc Ergo Propter Hoc*
Stories by Jason Brown, Bryan Charles, Amber Dermont, Luis Jaramillo, Dawn Raffel, Bryan Charles, Nina Shope, and Alicia Erian. Robert Olen Butler's severed heads. Poetry by Jim Harrison, Sarah Gorham, Trevor Dannatt, Matthew Rohrer & Joshua Beckman, and Harvey Shapiro. Art by Bill Adams, Juliana Ellman, Sally Ross, and George Rush. Eerie, illustrated children's story by Rick Rofihe and Thomas Roberston. Saucy cover by Wayne Gonzales. ($10)

*Homecoming*
"The Egg Man" a novella by Scott Smith, author of *A Simple Plan* (screenplay and book); Ryan Kenealy does God's math; an unpublished essay by Paul Bowles. Stories by Rachel Sherman, Sam Shaw, and Maxine Swann. Art by Shelter Serra and William McCurtin (of *Story of My Scab* and *Elk* fame). Poems by Anthony Roberts, Honor Moore, and David Lehman. ($10)

**Ballast**
Matthew Zapruder's "The Pajamaist," David Nutt's "Melancholera," fiction by Rachel Sherman, a Nick Tosches poem, Phillip Lopate's "Tea at the Plaza," David A. Fitschen on life on tour as a roadie. Poetry by Matt Miller and Alex Phillips. Art by Molly Smith, Robert Selwyn, Miranda Lichtenstein, Lorenzo Petrantoni, Billy Malone, and M Blash. ($10)

ISSUE #21

**Fiction/Nonfiction**
A special double-sided issue featuring fiction by Sam Lipsyte, Jerry Stahl, Herbert Gold, Leni Zumas, Matthew Kirby, Jonathan Baumbach, Ann Hillesland, Manuel Gonzales, and Leland Pitts-Gonzales. Nonfiction by Priscilla Becker, Vestal McIntyre, Eric Pape, Jocko Weyland, and Vince Passaro. ($10)

ISSUE #22

**Prose by Poets**
Prose and poetry by Anne Sexton, Nick Flynn, Jim Harrison, Wayne Koestenbaum, Joe Wenderoth, Glyn Maxwell, Rebecca Wolff, Vijay Seshadri, Jerome Badanes, Deborah Garrison, Jill Bialosky, Cynthia Kraman, Max Blagg, Thorpe Moeckel, Greg Purcell, Rodney Jack, Hadara Bar-Nadav, and Nancy Willard. ($10)

ISSUE #23

**Secret Engines**
Three debuts: Malerie Willens, Gerard Coletta, and Ian Martin. Stanley Moss as a bronze satyr; heavy breathing with Jeff Johnson. Stories by Jonathan Baumbach, Erin Brown, Wayne Conti, James Hannaham, and Claire Keegan. Poetry by Mark Hartenbach, Alex Lemon, and Baron Wormser. Art by Amy Bird, Jay Batlle, Noelle Tan, and Doug Shaeffer. ($10)

ISSUE #24

**High Wire**
Robert Stone's epic novella (set midway between the reigns of Elvis Presley and Bill Clinton); stories by Jonathan Ames, Charles Bukowski, Rivka Galchen, Jon Groebner, Said Shirazi, Giuseppe O. Longo, and Sarah Gardner Borden. Poetry by Howard Altmann, Jennifer Richter, and Ben Carlton Turner. Art by Ellen Harvey, Michael Scoggins, Mark C, and Duncan Hannah. ($10)

ISSUE #25

# CITY

Please send a check or money order payable to:

Open City, Inc.
270 Lafayette Street, Suite 1412
New York, NY 10012

For credit-card orders, see www.opencity.org.

*The New Soft Shoe*
Brad Gooch on Flannery O'Connor at Iowa; stories by Kirsty Gunn, Mohammed Naseehu Ali, Matthew Specktor, Caedra Scott-Flaherty, Henry Alcalay, and Chris Spain. Poetry by Priscilla Becker, William Benton, John Fandel, Christopher Kang, Strawberry Saroyan, and Elizabeth Schmidt. Gorgeous collage cover by Balint Zsako. ($10)

*Birthmark*
Patricia Bosworth on Lois Gould, Edmund White on Harold Brodkey. Stories by A. M. Homes, Vestal McIntyre, and Zachary Lazar; nonfiction by Bryan Charles; a posthumous fiction debut by Eva Marer. Poetry by Billy Collins, Dara Weir, and CJ Evans. Stunning cover and art project by Karen Green; art projects by Eliott Puckette, Louise Despont, Audrey Salmon, and Christopher de Lotbinière. ($10)

# SUBSCRIBE

One year (3 issues) for $30; two years (6 issues) for $55.
Add $10/year for Canada & Mexico; $20/year for all other countries.

Please send a check or money order payable to:
Open City, Inc.   270 Lafayette Street, Suite 1412   New York, NY 10012
For credit-card orders, see www.opencity.org.

# The Bitch of This Exchange

## Sam Lipsyte

AMERICA, SAID HORACE, THE OFFICE TEMP, WAS A RUN-DOWN and demented pimp. Our republic's whoremaster days were through. Whither that frost-nerved, diamond-fanged hustler who'd stormed Normandy, dick-smacked the Soviets, turned out such firm emerging market flesh? Now our nation slumped in the corner of the pool hall, some gummy coot with a pint of Mad Dog and soggy yellow eyes, just another mark for the juvenile wolves.

"We're the bitches of the First World," said Horace, his own eyes braziers of delight.

We all loved Horace, his clownish pronouncements. He was a white kid from Armonk who had learned to speak and feel from a half-dozen VHS tapes in his father's garage. Besides, here at our desks with our turkey wraps, I did not disagree.

But I let him have it. It was my duty. We were in what they call a university setting. A bastion of, et cetera. Little did I know this was my last normal day at said bastion, that my old friend Purdy was about to butt back into my world, mangle it. I just figured this was what my worst teachers used to call a teachable moment.

"Horace," I said. "That's a pretty sexist way to frame a discussion of America's decline, don't you think? Not to mention racist."

"I didn't mention anybody's race," said Horace.

"You didn't have to."

"P.C. robot."

"Fascist dupe."

"Did you get avocado on yours?"

"Fattening," I said.

"Don't worry, baby," said Horace. "I like big women."

"What about hairy ones?" I said, parted my shirt to air my nipple fuzz. Horace let me be a cretin with him. You could call him my infantilism provider, though you'd sound like an idiot. Otherwise, I was ostensibly upstanding, a bald husband, a slab-bellied father.

"Gentlemen," said our supervisor, Vargina, coming out from her command nook. "Did you send off those e-mails about the Belgian art exchange?"

Horace swiveled back to his monitor with the mock panic of a sitcom serf. Vargina took scant notice of our talk, tolerated foul banter for purposes of morale. But the fact remained, we had forgotten the afternoon's assignment. The gods of task flow did not easily forgive.

Where we worked was in the development office of a mediocre university in New York City. It was an expensive and strangely obscure institution, named for its syphilitic Whig founder, but we often called it, with what we considered a certain panache, the Mediocre University *at* New York City. By we, I mean Horace and I. By often, I mean once.

Our group raised funds and materials for the university's arts programs. People paid vast sums so their spawn could take hard drugs in suitable company, draw from life on their laptops, do radical things with video cameras and caulk. Still, the sums didn't quite do the trick. Not in the cutthroat world of arts education. Our job was to grovel for more money. We could always use more video cameras, more caulk, or a dance studio, or a gala for more groveling. The asks liked galas, openings, recitals, shows. They liked dinner with a famous filmmaker for them to fawn over or else dismiss as frivolous.

An ask could be a person, or what we wanted from that person. If they gave it to us, that was a give. The asks knew little about the student work they funded. Who could blame them? Some of the art these brats produced wouldn't stand up to the dreck my three-year-old son Bernie demanded we tack to the kitchen wall. But I was biased, and not just because I often loved my son. Thing was, I'd been just like these wretches once. Now they stared through me, as though I were merely some drone in their sight line, a pathetic object momentarily obstructing their fabulous horizon. They were right. That's exactly what I was.

A solitudinous roil, my bitterness. Horace, after all, was their age. He had no health insurance, just hope. Our rainmaker, Llewellyn, seemed born to this job, keen for any chance to tickle the rectal bristles of the rich with his Tidewater tongue. He was almost never in the office, instead sealing the deal on a Gulfstream IV to Bucharest, or lying topside on a Corfu yacht, slathered in bronzer.

Llewellyn delivered endowed chairs, editing suites, sculpture gardens. My record was not so impressive. My last big ask, for example, had failed to yield a few plasma TVs from the father of a recent film graduate.

Mr. Ramadathan had mortgaged his electronics store so his son could craft affecting screenplays about an emotionally distant, workaholic immigrant's quest for the American dream. But the father's giddiness had begun to wear off. The boy was unemployable. Now Mr. Ramadathan was maybe not so eager to relinquish his showroom models.

I'd made the hot, khaki-moistening hike past all the car dealerships and muffler shops on Northern Boulevard in Queens, stood in the sleek, dingy cool of the store. Mr. Ramadathan sat near the register in a wicker chair. The plasmas were not on display. Sold or hidden, I had no idea. Mr. Ramadathan stared at me, at the sweat patches on my crotch. He pointed toward some old video game consoles, a used floor fan, dregs of the dream.

"Please," he said, "take those. So that others may learn."

Unlike the time Llewellyn secured a Foley stage for the film department, there was no celebration on the Mediocre patio. No sour chardonnay got guzzled in my honor, nor did any lithe director of communications flick her tongue in my ear, vow to put me on the splash page of *Excellence*, the university's public relations blog.

If not so ecstatic in her position as Llewellyn, Vargina seemed happy enough, or at least adopted a mode of wise, unruffled decency in the office. She'd been a crack baby, apparently due to her mother being a crackhead, one of the early ones, the baking soda vanguard. Vargina was a miracle, and that's maybe the only time I have used the word sincerely. Her mother had named her the word her name resembled. A sympathetic nurse added the "r."

"Milo," she said now. "How is the Teitelbaum ask going?"

Vargina had enormous breasts I liked to picture flopping out of a sheer burgundy bra. Sometimes they just burst out in slow motion. Sometimes she scooped them out with her slender hands, asked me to join her reading group.

"Making progress," I said. "Chipping away."

"Maybe you need a larger tool," said Vargina, appeared to shudder slightly, perhaps worried her innocent metaphor would be misconstrued as sexual. Her words, however, were not misconstrued at all. I had already begun to picture my cock in high quiver, sliding up the lubed swell of her chest. We were in a library of lacquered wood. Viola tones rose from a carved alcove. Baby oil beaded on rare folios.

"Well," said Vargina, tapped the plastic parapet of my cube wall. "Just stick with it."

"Will do."

Truth was, the Teitelbaum ask was going nowhere. I was barely hanging on here in development. I wasn't developing. I'd done some good work at a nonprofit a few years ago, but the South Bronx Restoration Comedy Project never really took off. The university snapped me up at a bargain rate. I'd become one of those mistakes you sometimes find in an office, a not unpleasant but mostly unproductive presence bobbing along on the energy tides of others, a walking reminder of somebody's error in judgment.

But today some karmic adjustment seemed due. Just as Vargina slipped back behind the particleboard walls of her command nook, a painting major we knew a bit too well around here charged up to my desk, planted her bony fist on my Vorticist mouse pad. McKenzie was one of those girls who didn't eat enough, so that all one really noticed about her were the mole-specked rods of her arms, the lurid jut of her skull. Students had no reason to visit our office, but her father had paid for our crappy observatory upstate. She was in here a lot, to preen, complain. I guess it beat making her putrid art.

"Hello, McKenzie," I said.

"Hi, yeah, sorry, I can't remember your name."

"Milo."

"Sure, okay. Milo. Listen, Milo, we talked last week and you promised I'd be able to take the Impressionism to Regressionism seminar even though it was full."

"Excuse me?"

"Yeah, you know, you promised you'd talk to the painting department and sort it all out. I mean, if I told my father—"

"Hold on."

"Hold on?"

"I made no such promise. We have nothing to do with academic decisions, with curriculum or enrollment."

"Okay, maybe it was that guy," said McKenzie, pointing.

"Horace?" I said.

"Yeah, Whore-Ass," said McKenzie.

Horace wore a pained grin at his terminal.

"Horace hasn't been well," I told McKenzie. "Now, as I mentioned, we have no jurisdiction over any of these issues, but maybe we can all get together with painting and figure this out."

"Meaning what?"

"Meaning we can figure this out."

McKenzie stared. How could she know I myself had once been a fraud, chockablock with self-regard, at an overpriced institution just like this one, still had the debt to prove it? How could she know she stared down at the wispy pate of a man who once believed he was painting's savior, back in a decade that truly needed one?

She spoke quietly now: "Listen, I don't mean to be rude, but you really are here to serve my needs. My father taught me that the consumer is always right. I am the consumer. You are actually the bitch of this particular exchange. But don't think I don't respect that you are just a guy, like, doing your shitty job."

"Thank you," I said.

"But maybe you aren't cut out to work with artists."

I guess what set me off was her effort to be polite. I should have just leaned on the painting department to make room on the roster for her, ruin the semester for some pimple-seared hump who shared his name with no stargazing facility. Nobody cared. I would be doing my shitty job. It was a good shitty job. I'd done it for a few years and it paid pretty well, enough to let Maura go part-time since the baby. There was a quality family plan, plus a quality theft plan, the paints and brushes I smuggled home for those weekends I tried to put something on canvas again, until the old agony would whelm me and I'd stop and briefly weep and then begin to drink and watch Maura cruise up and down the cable dial all night, never alighting on anything for more than a moment, her thumb poised like a hairless and tiny yet impressively predatory animal above the arrow button, Maura herself bent on peeking into every corner of the national hallucination before bedtime.

She liked reality shows the best, and then the shows that purported to be about reality.

So, yes, I should have just surrendered, cinched the entitled scion her little pouch of entitlements, put in my calls to the name shufflers, done my duty.

I thought about that moment later on. Maybe I got extratuned to the concept of bitchhood once I became Purdy's, though I must confess I've always found such usage of the term for female dogs distasteful. My mother was a second-wave feminist. I wasn't comfortable saying "cunt" until I was twenty-three, at which point, admittedly, I couldn't hold back for a time.

Or maybe it's just that I've always despised phrases like "that fateful day," but as time went on I found it hard to deny that the afternoon Horace launched his E Pluribus Pimpus oratory and McKenzie tried to reify my servility and I pictured titboning Vargina in a rare books room was pretty damn fateful. Or was it, in fact, just another random day, and it was I who did the fool thing, forced my hand?

What I said to McKenzie, there is no point repeating. It's enough to report my words contained nothing an arrogant, talentless, daddy-damaged waif wants to hear about herself. When I was finished she did not speak. A thickish vein in her pale head fluttered. The blue thing seemed to veer and switch direction. Then she took a few steps back and, still staring at me, phoned her damager. What was done to me was done in hours. My outburst was deemed hate speech, which called for immediate dismissal. I could hardly argue with them. I think it probably was hate speech. I really fucking hated that girl.

Home, hidden by the refrigerator, I hovered over the garbage bin, gulped down a bottle of Vitamin Drink. We still dreaded the day that little Bernie, asquat now on the kitchen floor spooning oatmeal into the body cavity of a decapitated superhero, might spot this iridescent liquid, demand a sip. Vitamin Drink may or may not have contained vitamins, but it was too polluted for the tykes. They needed wholesome nectars humped back from the wholesome food empires in Manhattan. This sugary shit was for the dying. I was dying, surely, sugary-ly.

I made to speak before I did.

"A call. A message. From work."

"What?" said Maura. "Work? What work?"

Maura sat on a stool, fresh from the shower and still unclothed, pecked at her laptop.

She had been raised in one of those happy, naked families from Vermont. I looked at her body now, remembered Bernie's weaning, that era of inconsolable sobs and farewell fondles. Maura's breasts, large and milk white when they'd been full of milk, had darkened, pancaked a bit, but they were still beautiful, and I was not just saying that, or thinking of saying that, to be kind.

"Wait," said Maura, "what?"

It was her I'm-downloading-a-crucial-file-from-the-office tone.

"A call from work on my voice mail," I said. "From old work. Vargina and Llewellyn. They want me to come in."

"Why would they want that?"

"I don't know."

"Wasn't firing you enough? Is this a legal thing? Do you need a lawyer?"

"I said I don't know."

I leaned out from my trash niche. Bernie pointed at the bottle in my hand.

"Daddy, what are you drinking?"

"Coffee, Bern. Why, do you think I need a lawyer?"

"Do lawyers have foreskins?" said Bernie.

"I'm talking to Mommy," I said.

"I have a foreskin."

"I know, Bernie."

"You don't."

"True," I said, opened the refrigerator door, sneaked the bottle back into the door rack.

"How come I have a foreskin, Daddy?"

"We've talked about this, don't you remember? Your mother and I decided that—"

"Hey, that's juice. I want some, Daddy! I want some juice!"

"Shit," I said. "Sorry. Bernie, it's not juice. It's for grown-ups. It's like coffee."

"You said it *was* coffee."

"That's right."

"But it's pink!"

"It's pink coffee, Bernie. It's what I drink. It's what grown-ups drink."

"Do superheroes have foreskins? Like my guy?"

He held up his headless hero.

"Yes. No. I don't know. Probably. So, who would I call, Maura? They want me tomorrow."

"Do they, Daddy?"

"I don't know, Bernie. It's possible."

"Do foreskins help you fly?"

"Maybe," I said.

"All I'm saying," said Maura, "is you don't have to play it their way. That's all you've ever done."

"Excuse me?" I said.

"Give me some juice!" Bernie called again. "I want it!"

"Ask nicely."

"Please."

"But it's not for kids, Bernie."

"Don't confuse him like that," said Maura. "Daddy's going to give Bernie some pink coffee juice that's not really coffee. Would Bernie like Daddy to give Bernie some pink coffee juice that's not really coffee? Daddy, would you please give Bernie some pink coffee juice that's not really coffee?"

"Fine!" I said.

"Fine!" said Bernie.

He flicked his guy and a cold gob of oatmeal slapped my cheek. I could see this was the beginning of something. Like sudden sympathy for Goliath. What was the phrase? Tell it not in Gath? How about we start telling it?

"What?" said Maura.

"Was I mumbling again?"

"Who's Goliath?" said Bernie. "A superhero? Is he a bad guy? A masher?"

"He's a masher, for sure," I said. "Whether he's a bad guy depends on your politics."

"What's politics?"

"Well, let me see. It's—"

"Does Goliath have a foreskin?"

"Not for long. Not when David's done with him."

"Who's David?"

"A foreskin collector."

"What are you telling him!" said Maura.

"Nothing," I said. "He should know about the Bible. He lives in a fucking theocracy."

"Jesus, language, Milo."

"Daddy! Juice!"

"Okay, Bern, but first, how about some water?"

I filled a cup from the tap. Bernie batted it away, lunged toward the refrigerator.

"Give me pink coffee juice, Daddy!"

"Okay," I said. "Okay."

I dumped out the tap water, took the Vitamin Drink from the refrigerator. Back turned, I mimed a long pour, added a drop for color, refilled the cup from the tap.

Bernie stared up at me.

"Let go, Dad," the boy seemed to be saying, but his beautiful mouth wasn't moving.

Later, in bed, Maura and I cuddled in the way of a couple about to not have sex. It never appeared to bother us much, unless we watched one of those cable dramas about a sexless marriage. Then we'd curse the inanity of the show, its implausibility, switch over to something where the human wreckage was too crass and tan to touch us.

"I still don't understand why they want to meet with you," said Maura.

"I don't, either. Maybe they realized they forgot to take the shirt off my back."

"It's not funny. That girl's father. I don't know."

"What more can they do to me?"

"Oh, I'm sure there are all sorts of things we'd never even think of."

"That's very calming. Thank you."

"I'm just saying. You never learned to protect yourself. You always rail against the evil and exploitation in the world but you still act as though everybody has your best interests at heart. I never got it. You're like an idiot savant without the savant part."

"I still have faith in the basic goodness of humanity. Shoot me."

"Don't be so sure that's not the plan."

Vargina had reserved the conference room. A tray of turkey wraps sat near the edge of the table. They looked like university wraps, from the cafeteria downstairs, not the deli across the street. They had no avocado.

Llewellyn and Vargina sat across the table. We took turns popping the tops of our sodas, listened to the sounds reverberate in the wood-paneled room. The word "reverberate" reverberated in my mind, which I could now picture as a wood-paneled room.

"It's nice to see you again," said Vargina.

"Hear, hear," said Llewellyn. "So, hoss, what have you been doing to yourself?"

"Excuse me?"

"Just shitting you," said Llewellyn. "Seriously, how's it going?"

"I didn't see Horace when I walked in," I said to Vargina.

"He's at a lunch."

"*A* lunch?"

"He's working on an ask."

"Horace? He's a temp."

"No longer," said Llewellyn. "He's looking like a little earner."

"Very exciting possibility, Horace's ask," said Vargina. "Very worthy. The lady is a major admirer of our dance program."

"Where's the money from?"

"Her husband's company. Private security. Military catering."

"Blood sausage, anyone?" I said.

"Oh, please," said Llewellyn. "We can't wash the bad off anybody's money, now, can we? But we can make something good out of all the misery. That's what you never understood."

"I understood it. I'm just not sure I believed it."

"Oh, some kind of martyr now, are you?"

"A martyr has to give a shit."

"Get over yourself, Milo. You're a sad man. A born wanker. You were born into the House of Wanker. You're a berk, and you probably think I'm just saying your last name."

Llewellyn's Cambridge year was the stuff of office legend, thanks to Llewellyn, but I'd always suspected he lifted most of his lingo from the British editions of American men's magazines.

"Wanker," I said. "Don't know that word. Is that a southern thing? What is that, Richmond? Newport News? Is that like peanuts in your Coke?"

"You have a provincial mind, hucklebuck."

"Pardon?"

"It's a global globe now," said Llewellyn. "We sink or swim together."

"It's a global globe?"

"That's right."

"Moron."

"Gentlemen," said Vargina.

"Why am I here?" I said. "I thought I was fired."

"You were," said Vargina.

"You are," said Llewellyn.

"Then what's going on?"

"We have special circumstances," said Vargina.

"You have special circumstances," I said.

"Yes."

"I have not-so-special circumstances," I said.

"If you help us with our circumstances," said Vargina, "we might be able to assist you with yours."

The door opened and in walked a large man with a moist pompadour and a tight beige mustache. Dean Cooley was not a dean. He was Mediocre's chief development officer. Several groups worked under him, and he spent most of his energy on the more lucrative ones, like business, law, or medicine. His art appreciation did not reach much past the impressionistic prints from the Montreal Olympics he'd mounted on his office wall. He'd been a marine, and then some kind of salesman, had started with cars and ended up in microchips and early internet hustles. Here in the cozy halls of academe, as he had put it during our first team talk, he meant to reassess his priorities. Meanwhile he would train us maggots how to ask asks and get gives. Cooley was a hard-charger who often began his reply to basic office queries by invoking "the lessons of Borodino." He was the kind of man you could picture barking into a field phone, sending thousands to slaughter, or perhaps ordering the mass dozing of homes. People often called him War Crimes. By people, I mean Horace and I. By often, I mean twice.

"Dean," said Vargina. "This is the man we were telling you about. Milo Burke."

"Nice to meet you."

We'd met a dozen times before, at lunches, cocktail receptions. He had stood beside me while his wife explained a project she'd embarked upon in her student days, something to do with Balinese puppets and social allegory.

"I assume you are wondering why, after being terminated for cause two months ago, we've asked you to come in," Cooley began.

"A fair assumption," I said.

"What you need to understand is that the incident with Mr. Rayfield's daughter was very serious. Mr. Rayfield is still angry. You made his daughter doubt herself, artistically. He had to buy her an apartment in Copenhagen so she could heal."

"I'm sorry, sir."

"The whole debacle nearly cost us a new, working telescope for our observatory."

"I do understand that."

"But what you also need to understand is that we are not simply some heartless, money-mad, commercial enterprise. We are partly that, of course, but we are also a compassionate and, yes, money-mad place of learning. And while we're on the topic of learning, we think people can learn from their mistakes. We believe in redemption."

"As long," said Llewellyn, "as it is not tied to a particular ideology or religious tradition and promotes inclusiveness."

"Is that from the handbook, Lew?" said Dean Cooley. "Anyway, the point is, we are a family."

"A family dedicated to furthering science and the humanities in an increasingly meaning-starved culture," said Vargina.

"Well put," said Dean Cooley.

"But may I remind us all," said Llewellyn, "that here in development our task is to raise money for said furthering. We can't hug all day. We've got to get out there and work."

"Also well put. Especially these days. We need every drop of philanthropy we can get. We must fasten our lips to the spigot and suck, so to speak. Which is where you come in, Mr. Burke."

"Pardon?"

"It's an ask," said Vargina.

"A big one," said Llewellyn. "Not quite Rayfield range, but big."

"Why me?" I said.

"Good question," said Vargina.

"Yes," said Cooley. "That is the question, as the Bard might say."

"The Bard?"

"What's so funny?" said Cooley.

"Nothing, sir," I said. "I just didn't know people still used that term."

"Well, I'm a people, Burke. Am I not?"

"Of course."

"If you prick me, do I not bleed, you scat-gobbling, mother-rimming prick?"

Occasionally Dean Cooley reverted to a vocabulary more suited to his marine years, but some maintained it was only when he felt threatened, or stretched for time.

"Yes, sir," I said.

"Trust me, Milo," said Llewellyn. "Nobody wants it to be you. You were nothing but dead weight since the day you arrived. Nobody respects you and your leering got on people's nerves."

"My leering?"

Vargina shrugged, tapped her pen against her legal pad.

"Listen," said Cooley. "I don't give a slutty snow monkey's prolapsed uterus for your office politics. The point is that Burke needs to come back and complete this mission."

"Why?" I said. "Why me?"

"It's the ask," said Vargina. "The ask demands it."

"Excuse me?"

"He says he knows you. His wife is an alumnus of our extension program and they want to be donors, but when he found out you were in our office, he requested your presence. He wants to work with somebody he trusts."

"Who is this person?" I said.

"His name is Stuart. Purdy Stuart. You do know him, don't you?"

"Yes. I know him."

I said nothing more, felt now like the boy in the fairy-tale book I often read to Bernie, the polite farmer's son who stands before the cruel ogre's castle.

Each time Bernie would ask: "Daddy, why does the boy have to knock on the door? Why can't he just turn around and go home?"

Each time I'd chuckle with stagey amusement, say: "Well, kid, if he didn't open the door, we wouldn't have a story, would we?"

Odds were good I was, in the final analysis, nothing but a scat gobbler from the House of Wanker.

"I mean," I said now, "I used to know him."

"Well, that's just swell," said Cooley, rose, petted his mustache with a kind of cunnidigital ardor.

"I'm late for another meeting," he said. "Tell our contestant what he's won."

The door clicked shut behind him. It did not reverberate.

"What have I won?" I said.

"Your old job back," said Vargina. "If you make this work."

"And if I don't?"

"You'll be finished," said Llewellyn. "Forever. Do we have clarity?"

"Obscene amounts."

Llewellyn stood, stalked off. It would not be the last I saw of him, I knew. The ogres, they just lurk behind those gnarled oak doors so ubiquitous in fairy-tale carpentry, wait for gentle lads to knock. Trolls, on the other hand, they must have a paging device. Either way, the odious is ever ready.

Vargina and I sat there for a while, a new, electric awkwardness in the room.

"Can you make it happen?" said Vargina.

"When have I ever disappointed you?"

"Nearly every day that we have worked together."

"Listen," I said. "I just want to apologize."

"For what?"

"For the leering."

"The leering?"

"You know. That stuff Llewellyn said."

"Don't apologize to me. Apologize to Horace."

"Horace?"

"He's the one who reported you. But don't worry. He wasn't vindictive. He just said he didn't understand why somebody would need to be in the closet in this day and age. At least around here."

"In the closet," I said.

"But he's a kid. He doesn't know how complicated these things can get."

"No," I said. "I guess he doesn't."

Shawn had a shelf of books on managing difficult people. "The thing with negotiating." He put down his wine glass and crossed his legs. "You have to go into any conversation knowing what you want."

"We were just talking."

"Nothing is just talking. Someone always comes out boss."

"Is that how you think?"

"I try to."

"So, what are we doing now?"

"Listen," he said. "You wanted my opinion."

(Malone, page 81)

# Moving in the Almost

Sophie Cabot Black

From some distance I have come
By the only way, past the church upon the hill,
The village clock and shuttered windows,

Down the street that leads to where you live,
To each house until it is the simple
Outline of where you might be;

From the road to the gate to the door,
From the door to the room to the bed.
In the bed the figure turning. The moon

Poured out. One finger to reach
The furthest edge until you wake and I look
Hard into your face as if never seen before

And it is enough to make you rise,
Leave behind the room, the door,
The gate click as you walk out

And follow me to where I go. Now it is you
Who enter until you are leaving. Back and forth
We move as if each time we will be done.

# Where We Are Being What We Made

the night undid the bed
while we followed the snake
perfect your feet at my head
my feet in your mouth as
if in some forest a clearing
held back not by fire but
by abandon
and how the end is all about
what we do not yet know
save how we are what we make
which means there is no place
to break what happens into
seeing it is enough

# Gate

Which cannot open
   with you on the other side,

That would not be
    your version, instead to say

It is the workman's fault;
   the last one gone, he who did not check

His own labor, by then already paid,
   and though you heard the truck leaving

You did not call him back,
   the day slowly ticked itself out

As you looked up at any sound
   by your window on the street

Stunned by each transaction
   not yours, the piano in the building beyond

Again and again
   trying to get it right,

Easier to just lie down
    not to sleep, but stay with the sky

## OPEN CITY

Of nothing happening
   and what you wanted to say, the voice

In the machine
   which will not be erased

Unless by mistake;
   it wants to be kept, heard each day

Through each message
   to find the new one, to go over

And over back into entering
   where you may not have begun but are in.

# The Privileges

## Jonathan Dee

AT SCHOOL APRIL'S FIRST TASK WAS TO ESTEEM HERSELF. THEY began with self-portraits, huge-headed, in which the bodies were an afterthought, apportioned roughly the same space on the page as a nose or an ear. The portraits smiled widely with crooked teeth, not because the children's teeth were crooked but because teeth were hard to draw. They made lists of the reasons they liked themselves, lists of the things they were good at and the things at which they were determined to improve. They named the comforts of their homes—pets, siblings, favorite toys, or favorite places. One girl said her favorite place was Paris, but April took this to mean the imaginary Paris of the Madeline books. Her own favorite place was her parents' bed, with her parents not in it, just her and a few stuffed animals and a juice box and a movie on DVD. She dreamed of this situation often, though in practice she usually had to be sick to attain it. Something told her, though, that it would be seen as babyish, and so she said the Central Park Carousel instead.

Less auspicious was the name project. A name, the students were told, had a secret history; it might connect you to the country from which your family had first emigrated, or to the language or the religion of that country, or even just to the family itself and the loved ones who had gone before. It let you know that you were not just some one-time phenomenon but an outcome, a culmination, the top branch of a majestic tree. Told to go home and conduct some re-search on why she was named April Morey, she saw her parents ex-change a quick look before her mother answered.

"Well," Cynthia said, muting the TV, "Dad and I talked about a lot of different names. We would sit on the couch in our old apartment and try them out on each other back when I was pregnant with you, say them out loud to see how they sounded. And there were a few we liked, but we kept coming back to April. April Morey. It just sounded the most beautiful to us."

Her dad smiled, and patted her mom's leg.

"That's it?" April asked.

They looked as confused as she was. "Also," her father said, sitting forward on the couch, "it's a pretty unusual name. Not a lot of other Aprils in the world. We wanted a name as special as you are."

They'd given her her name not because somebody else had had it, but because nobody had? "Was there ever another April in our fam-ily?" she asked. They looked at each other again, and shook their heads. "Why didn't you name me after a loved one?"

"A loved one?" Adam said.

April nodded. "A dead loved one. That's what a lot of people do. Or somebody from the old country." Her mother punched her father in the thigh, and that, it shocked April to realize, was because he had been about to laugh.

"Where do we come from?" she demanded of them. "What coun-try?"

Stunningly, they seemed less than sure. Adam knew his father's family had come from England, but he didn't know where in England specifically, nor how many generations ago that had been; his moth-er's family was part German and part Dutch. Cynthia knew her father's ancestors were Russian, unless he'd been lying about that too, and as for her maternal grandparents, her mother had always refused to discuss them.

"Was there something special about the *month* of April?" April asked. There wasn't. No historic event had taken place then, no an-niversary or birthday, though they did offer that if April's birthday had actually fallen in April, they would have named her something else.

"What would you have named me instead?" she demanded. The revelation that she, April, might just as plausibly have been Samantha or Josephine or Emma, that only chance was behind the whole solemn question of her identity, made her feel worse than ever. She could see that her parents were now upset, but she was angry at them and didn't care. They kept coming back to beauty, but it was a beauty she couldn't comprehend and that she wasn't at all sure her teacher would consider a satisfactory completion of the assignment.

Ms. Diaz was nice about it, of course, but there was nothing to be done about the jealousy engendered by the other, longer name-essays that went up on the walls above their lockers, stories of honored relatives and cool languages and religious rituals tended through the generations. April felt as if her family came from nowhere, and, more puzzlingly, that this suited her parents just fine.

The next unit was family traditions. The teacher took pains to define this idea as broadly as possible; still, what traditions did April's family have? They hardly ever did the same thing even twice. They had no ancestral home they returned to, no church they attended (her mom had gone to church as a child but April had heard her say that she hated it and was glad she never had to go again), no special place they liked to travel to—indeed, having been someplace on vacation once, like Nantucket or Vail or Disney World, even if they'd had a good time there, was usually cited as a reason not to go there again. Even their Christmas tree wasn't in the same spot every year. April knew her own grandparents so little that she sometimes mixed them up in her head and was shy about talking to them on the phone. She had one uncle and no aunts, just something her mother called a stepaunt, whom she'd only ever seen in a photo in her parents' wedding album.

Soon the whole temper of the assignment had changed, in April's mind, from an exercise in self-discovery to an indiscriminate hunt for what Ms. Diaz, for whom she would have died in any case, wanted to admire in her. It seemed perfectly defensible to start making things up. She wrote down that her family went to Saint Patrick's Cathedral every Sunday, and that they were considering a trip to Jerusalem for Christmas. Her grandmother on her mother's side, who was named May, had lost her parents as a girl but had gamely made her way from Holland to America by boat. Every summer April and her cousins gathered for a reunion at the family estate on a mountain in New Hampshire. It was so big that some of her distant, pioneer relatives were buried in a small graveyard right there on the place.

Adam and Cynthia read these notions on the wall beneath their daughter's self-portrait on Parents' Night, mute with amazement. April's teacher couldn't really believe this stuff, could she? Yet she had posted it right there with all the other handwritten, dubiously spelled histories of persistence and hardship. They already felt conspicuous, as they always did at these school functions, as the youngest couple in the classroom; at twenty-nine they were still strikingly young, by Manhattan standards at least, to be parents at all. Jonas's best friend in kindergarten had once slept over for a whole weekend while his father took his mother to London for her fiftieth birthday. Every Parents' Night Adam and Cynthia were a kind of generation unto themselves, and it didn't take much, in that context, to awaken a vestigial unease about being in some sort of trouble they didn't even understand. When Ms. Diaz, deep in conversation with some kid's father who was surely old enough to be their father too, smiled at them from across the room as if to say that she would be with them in just a moment, they smiled back warmly until she turned away and then Cynthia squeezed Adam's arm and they got the hell out of there.

When she'd first stopped working outside the home, as the expression went, the kids were toddlers with unsynchronized nap schedules and so Cynthia's brain was pretty much indentured to them; even apart from the physical exhaustion, it was a struggle just to find a little interior space for herself, a little space in which to *be* herself, when they were so present and so vulnerable and so demanding every minute of the day. The only time that truly felt like her own was late at night when everyone else was asleep, when she would stay up and watch movies and savor the day's one cigarette, blowing the smoke out the window; but even that came at a price, since the sleep she lost made the next day's selflessness harder to maintain.

But now they were older, the school day was longer, and she determined that she could pick up where she left off and start working again. She took this idea more literally than she would have if she'd thought about it more. Her first and only job in New York, from the summer after college until after Jonas was born, had been as an editorial assistant at a glossy, ad-heavy magazine called *Beauty,* and in the absence of any other sort of work she particularly burned to do, she thought she might go back there. It was a painful miscalculation. Her best memories of *Beauty* were mostly memories of the kind of euphoric bitching that took place over drinks after work with her fellow assistants; most of those smart young women and gay men were now, like Cynthia, long gone, but a couple had stuck it out and managed to rise up the masthead. That was the only way to get anything decent out of a career in magazines—become a lifer. The current features editor was someone she used to eat cheap lunches with back when they were happy to get through the day without getting screamed at by someone important. Her name was Danielle. Cynthia left a message with Danielle's assistant, got a call back from a different assistant asking her to come in the following Monday at eleven-thirty, and arrived to find Danielle standing up behind her desk with a look of awkward condescension on her narrow face that said everything there was to say.

Still, they had to go through with it. Cynthia, angry and humiliated and eager to leave before Danielle had even sat down again, produced pictures of April and Jonas. Danielle told the story of her own broken engagement. They recalled some of the people they had worked with back in the day. Cynthia had no idea what had happened to any of them; Danielle knew what had happened to all of them. It was possible to connect the overbearing power chick she was now to the emotionally manipulable peon she had been back then, but just barely. Finally they came with mutual reluctance to the subject at hand.

"Come on," Cynthia found herself saying. "I'm smart and I work hard and I can tell a good idea from a shitty one. If that was true five years ago it can't be untrue now. Children don't actually make you stupid—you do know that, right? Or maybe that would make a good investigative piece for you."

What kept her there past the point of good sense was her imagination of the dismayed, relieved, pitying expression into which Danielle's face would resolve the moment her office door closed between them. She postponed that moment as long as she could, even when doing so came off as begging. "You don't want what I can offer you," Danielle kept saying, and she was right, Cynthia didn't want it, but even less did she want to be spoken to like a child by someone who used to be her peer and now presumed to tell her what she did or did not want. In the end, in a thoroughly bridge-burning mood, she wrote "eat me" across the top of the résumé she'd brought, slid it across Danielle's desk, and walked out.

On the street she had a sudden memory, useless now, of a night out after work six or seven years ago when Danielle had gotten so drunk—Cynthia, pregnant by then, was stone sober—that she'd started hitting on the troll of a bartender and Cynthia was deputed to take her home in a cab. The bed in her York Avenue studio, which Cynthia had never visited before, was covered with stuffed dogs. But it wasn't surprising that Danielle should have changed. There was a fast-moving mainstream in life, and once you'd dropped out of it, as Cynthia had, you weren't going to be hailed by everybody when you tried to step into it again.

That was what had happened to her: she had fallen into the underworld of women with nothing vital to do. Like those moms she despised, the ones you made small talk with while you waited for your kid to find his shoes after a playdate at their Versailles-like apartments, who had live-in help and no real responsibilities and yet all they did was complain about how they never had a moment to themselves. But what filled Cynthia's days? She was at the gym five mornings a week now; Adam kept telling her she looked hotter than she ever had in her life, which was probably true, but maybe the whole routine there wasn't even about that, maybe it was about something else entirely. She had volunteered, again, to head the silent-auction committee for April's grade and for Jonas's too, even though she took no pleasure in it because of the proximity it forced her into with women whom she imagined were nothing like her. She had a rule about not drinking before five. She never broke it, but why was it there at all?

She and Adam joked all the time about the social purgatory to which they'd condemned themselves by having kids so young: some of their old friends were still hooking up in bars and setting up Hamptons shares, while the people who actually lived the same sort of domesticated life the Moreys lived tended to be a dozen years older, boring as hell, and too covetous of their youth to befriend them in any case. They'd go to some school function and after a couple of drinks all the middle-aged Wall Street husbands would be hitting on her; she thought it was hilarious, and Adam did too, and then the next day their fat-ass wives would make a point of not talking to her, as if that was supposed to be some sort of punishment. Still, her own charisma had become latent in her; who were her friends now?

Her erstwhile maid of honor, Marietta, was one of those with whom Cynthia had lost touch, all the more disgracefully since she lived right there in Tribeca—more than a hundred blocks away, but still. She was married now, to some Viacom executive she had met at a speed-dating event—you had to hand it to her, she embraced all that stuff, the newer it was the more unintimidated she felt—but married or not it was hard to stay in contact with her because she worked ten or twelve hours a day as vice president of a media-relations company, one of those places that orchestrated the public rehabilitation of the disgraced: drunk starlets, politicians who turned up in sex videos, clients like that. "It's a lot like being a lawyer," was how Marietta had explained it to her. "Or a lot like advertising. It's a lot like most things, actually." As if to prove their bond, just when Cynthia was missing her most Marietta called one night out of nowhere and begged Cynthia to meet her for a drink the next afternoon: there was something she needed to ask her. Cynthia said that, since she had to pick up the kids from school at three-thirty, maybe coffee was better. "Fuck that," Marietta said. "We'll have drinks at two, then. It's not like it's unprecedented. Remember that time at Head of the Charles when we made martinis at nine in the morning?"

"Less than distinctly," Cynthia said, smiling.

She actually wondered whether Marietta was going to offer her a job, weird as that would be, but instead it turned out that she was trying to get pregnant. She and Mr. Viacom had only been at it for six months but Marietta, who at thirty was a less patient person than she used to be, was getting ready to start on clomiphene. "How did it happen with you?" she asked Cynthia. "When it happened, I mean like the moment it happened, did you just know?"

"Don't you remember?" Cynthia said. "It was a total fucking shock. I was on my honeymoon. I'm still not sure how it happened."

"What about with Jonas?" she said, biting a cuticle. "Were you trying there?"

"Nope."

She scowled. "Fertile bitch. Well, you're still the only friend I can talk to about any of this who wouldn't try to talk me out of it. If they got wind of it at work, forget about it."

They sat at an outdoor table at a café across from the entrance to the Met, drinking lemon-drop martinis. There was no one else in the place at that hour but their waiter, and even he was barely in evidence.

"Here's the big discovery," Marietta said. "Here's the one aspect of this subject about which I know more than you. Sex when you're *trying* to get pregnant is the absolute worst sex known to man. Another six weeks of this and I swear to God if I'm not knocked up we're going to get divorced."

"Come off it," said Cynthia. Her new martini was too full to lift without spilling, so she was hunched over in her chair trying to sip from it.

"They always tell you that this is the true calling of sex, right? The higher purpose. It should be beautiful. Two people in love trying to create a new life. And let me tell you, it is easily the most joyless humping I've ever been a part of in my entire life. Remember Tom Billings?"

Cynthia thought for a moment. "From freshman orientation?" she said.

Marietta nodded ominously. "*That* was better than this," she said. "I just want him to come already and get out of the room so I can lie there like an idiot holding my knees up in the air like I'm supposed to. You'd think it's a guy's dream, right? Just blow your load and get out. But no: he wants to act like he's in some kind of weird Christian porno, going really slowly, stroking my hair, telling me that he loves me. Jesus!" She looked at Cynthia for a frozen moment, her mouth open in amazement, and then she started to laugh. "And he knows what I'm thinking, and I do feel sorry for him, but at the same time if this is all too hard on his fucking *ego,* well boo hoo. The last time we did it we didn't even say a word to each other until the next day. Speaking of which," she said, pulling her phone out of her purse, "I should give him a call. Today is supposed to be one of our prime fertility days. He has to come straight home from work and inseminate me, and if he's forgotten, I'll kill him. Excuse me a minute. Two more?" she said to the waiter.

By the time they finished the next round, they were both laughing so hard that they had to steal napkins from the empty tables around them to wipe away tears, drawing stares from the pedestrians who passed in the sunlight just beyond the awning. Half an hour later they had hugged goodbye three times and vowed to see each other more often and Cynthia, drunk and paranoid, was on her way to Dalton to pick up the kids. She'd have to avoid conversation with the other mothers, but since they didn't like her anyway, there wasn't much trick to that. As for the kids, they weren't old enough, she reassured herself, to be able to tell; besides, this being Tuesday, April had dance and Jonas had tee ball so it was just a matter of rushing them into a cab and racing around the east side anyway. No worries about making conversation. The kids hated it when they were late for things.

She remembered walking up this same stretch of Fifth Avenue years ago, when Jonas was still an infant, and as she waited for the light to change, one of those overly sunny old ladies who felt free to accost you whenever you were pushing a stroller had started pointing and cooing at him. When she was done she gazed up at Cynthia and said, "Enjoy this time. It goes by so fast," and Cynthia said, Well then either my watch has stopped or one of us is nuts. Or maybe she hadn't actually said that out loud. She couldn't remember anymore.

That had been a tough time, with both kids still in diapers. Still, even now, probably her dirtiest secret was that impatience for these years to be over: for them to be teenagers, at least, where they started to fend for themselves a little bit and where she wouldn't have to spend so much time wondering whether she would prove equal to whatever bad thing might befall them. Most days were fine, but then once in a while she would feel herself caught in an afternoon that just seemed to refuse to pass. On the bright side, they were way ahead of most children their age, and part of that had to be that she made more than just a cameo appearance in their daytime lives, that unlike so many of their friends they weren't being raised by nannies who ferried them dispassionately from place to place like they were especially valuable packages. She didn't care whether or not they appreciated that now but some part of her was counting on their appreciating it later. And she hated it when people handed you that Norman Rockwell shit about kids growing up too fast; on the contrary, she looked forward to being able to talk to them almost as peers, maybe ask their advice once in a while instead of feeling like she had to have all the answers all the time. Anyway, when you considered the whole bazaar of damage that childhood exposed you to, was there even any such thing as growing up too fast?

She checked her watch again; she'd checked it just a few seconds ago, but somehow five minutes had gone by, and she quickened her pace. She didn't want to get there after the bell. Walking in the bright sunlight gave her a piercing headache, sort of like being drunk and hung over at the same time. As she searched her bag again for the sunglasses she already knew she'd left on the hall table at home, she heard a voice through the uncomfortable buzz inside her head, a voice that whispered, *too late. Too late.*

Which was ridiculous. She was barely thirty. At Adam's old job there was a broker who used to be a professional dog walker, who graduated from business school at age thirty-five. Too late for what, exactly? It might have made a difference if there were some type of work she felt passionate about, or some particular skill she might cultivate into excellence, something a little more marketable than just above-average intelligence and fear of idleness. Marietta loved to make fun of her dissolute clients, but if you got her drunk enough she would start talking in dead earnest about her job in terms of second chances and the desire to repent. Well, if you got Cynthia drunk enough, Cynthia thought, she would cop to wanting to do some good in the world, or at least to feel like her presence in it was value-added. How, though? Without some framework, some resources, even your secret aspirations just curdled into sentimental bullshit.

A lot of time seemed to have gone by very suddenly. The injustice of it, the knowledge that one could never go back to where one had started, to the old advantages, didn't subside that day or the next. She knew that, every day, some woman somewhere did exactly what now seemed so impossible to her. Nevertheless she persisted in feeling that some sort of privilege had been stolen from her, not by the children, of course, but by someone.

"It's not a diagnosis, Toller.

These are colloquial expressions in everyday use.

When someone tells someone else that a third person they both know is paranoid or antisocial everyone's clear on the meaning."

(Sorrentino, page 51)

# Toby Dead

## Laurie Stone

AT EIGHTY-NINE, MY MOTHER LEARNS THAT HER ARTERIES ARE clogged with plaque like tubes with toothpaste, but she brushes off the news and goes into cardiac arrest. A squat little machine that looks like R2-D2 is attached to her by a vacuum cleaner hose, and my sister is holding a clipboard. Ellen is tapping it with a long, hard fingernail saying, "You have two choices, Ma, sign the form or dead. Which is it, Ma, the form or dead?" I am glancing from the machine to my mother, who looks like a chimp caught in a lab experiment. She trains her beady eyes on Ellen, as if she's being conned, but she takes the pen in her monkey paw and signs on for three more years of life—as well as a stroke and the twenty-four-hour care of home aides. My mother and I don't like each other, don't see eye to eye, don't get along, but love is somewhere in the room. I feel responsible for her no matter what. It's like watching your own death.

The last time I see her, she's a pile of sticks in the hospital. "Get away," she screams at the sight of me, so loud the woman in the next bed pleads with me to stop her. "How?" I ask, "I'm open to suggestions."

We don't pick who we love. We don't pick who we don't love. People say: I'm sorry for your loss, but what is my loss? When I am thirty-five and my father is dying of liver cancer, my mother sends me to the hospital, then blames me for his death. At nineteen, as I am walking to my wedding, she tells me to go get killed because Bruce's parents want their friends at the ceremony and I'm fine with that. Do your life passages play out operatic, or are they civilized, like in *Our Town*? Everyone has stories. Some people let go of them like stones from their pockets. Some people keep them because it's what they have.

When I am little and crossing streets, my mother and I squeeze hands in pulse beats. We live in Washington Heights, near St. Nicholas Avenue, and it is a river of shops and strangers, foreign words, sausages wrapped in greasy paper and eaten on the fly. We are moving, and we are together. My sister is at school, my father at work, and Toby and I are on the streets. People talk to us. Strangers talk to my mother. She is beautiful with deep-set eyes and high cheekbones, clip clopping in high heels and pencil skirts, and there is something about her. She says more than she needs to at the butcher's, so he paints a picture of his kids or the in-laws. He is ready to talk when we arrive, hands me a little sandwich of salami on rye with a smear of mustard. Toby prefers strangers to most people—strangers on buses, at the Automat, in the park. She can say anything. What can it hurt? In the morning, I watch from her bed as she drifts around naked, splashing on My Sin, attaching nylons to dangling garters. She will take me to the park to shovel sand, but it's the streets she's after, clip clopping, and she's waiting for Ellen. My mother can't juggle two friends, and Ellen is first. You can tell by the way they exchange looks in the school yard and how they laugh at things I will still not understand by the time Toby dies and I am sixty-one.

In Long Beach, Long Island, we have dinners out. While the rest of us share, my mother eats her own portion of roast pork with Chinese vegetables. It's bok choy, but we don't know the name. Long Beach is not a city. You drive from here to there. When my father and sister are away, I will go anywhere with my mother, even though I can't tell if she is happy or sad. We drift to shopping malls where there are stores and strangers but no streets. She's dying to get lost. I adore her. She embarrasses me. She will say someone is ugly so they can hear her. I want to look like her. I spend as much time as I can sleeping at my friend Linda's house. When I am five, I go to sleep-away camp for two months for the first time. I miss her. I thrive. When she visits, she reaches out for Ellen first. "Because she's older," Toby says.

The Toby of Long Beach is backing up a finned, yellow Pontiac, looking over her shoulder with a cigarette twisted in her lips. We're headed to the Malibu Beach Club, and I am fat. Outside her cabana, my mother—wearing a turquoise halter, her shoulders bronzed—moves mahjong pieces in a home movie. In the late afternoon, she pads to the ocean where waves lap her copper legs and foam surrounds her trim waist. Each splash is a shock because she has never learned to swim. She tells strangers about the time my father rigged a float behind a rowboat and Ellen, then a toddler, slipped out and almost drowned. "She turned blue," my mother says to anyone on the sand.

She sits across from me at Starbucks, her hair fluffy and white—a color close to her platinum bleach jobs. She's out of her wheelchair, on a wooden seat, spooning up a Frappucino and licking her lips. "I never eat between meals. I'm only doing it to please you." I broach the subject of money. Usually I don't ask her for things, but she's given my sister her diamond ring worth forty thousand dollars, while I have received nothing. I'm commuting to Arizona because I've fallen in love with a Brit named Richard. We met at an artist colony, and he teaches museum studies in Phoenix. I am sixty and I want my mother to be nice. We want what we want. I propose she give me five thousand dollars a year for four years, half the value of the ring. She narrows her eyes, and her head snaps back. "I won't give you anything."

I'm not surprised. Money is what my mother has, the way she used to have beauty—a little leverage, a little bait. She can reward my sister, because Ellen's love isn't in question, and anyway Ellen can't be tantalized because she has plenty of loot of her own. Toby can see yearning on my face—or maybe it's love—and it unnerves her that I can't wipe it off. She doesn't want to be reminded she prefers one child to the other, doesn't want to be that kind of mother. Generally, she likes talking about money—how much you earn, when it could run out. I like talking about money, too; money is desire before it's transformed into something that can disappoint you. I want her jewelry and the little bowls she sets on tables. I want her things the way I want her.

She tries to stand but can't, and I feel her entrapment. She's bellowing, and we're getting fidgety looks. I suggest we talk about something else—Ellen's grandchildren or the biography of Harry Truman she's reading. Why does she admire Truman? I'm not going to get into it. She doesn't think it matters he dropped the bomb. It wasn't on her people.

She squints, pushing aside her drink and reaching for her walking stick, her good arm shaking, her back twisting into a C shape. I help her stand, and she leans into me with distaste. Because we're touching? Because I can still walk? She tells me how to position my feet, move the chair, and lock the wheels, as if I've never performed these tasks before. The chair takes on an alien aspect, and I forget to swing aside the foot rests to allow her a clear path. As she shuffles forward, she nearly falls, and we sway like drunken lovers at the end of a tango—a broken double act, Dean and Jerry embracing and looking daggers. I laugh. When Toby is tickled, her nostrils quiver and her eyes tear. She once accidentally clipped her sable scarf to my winter coat, and when I arrived at school and saw the furry snake poking out of a sleeve, I called her and she fell on the floor. She plops her backside onto the seat and squirms. I slip my hands under her armpits, feeling the boneless dough of her, and I hoist her up until she's settled. All the way back to her apartment, she shouts curses, wishing me to be shot or run over by a car, chin up, so her voice rains down on me. Passersby stare. What does she care? I get a helicopter view of us rolling east on Fifty-seventh Street: a shrunken old woman in a worn brown hat and her sixty-year-old daughter in need of some Botox.

I once e-mailed a man on a dating site and when I disclosed my name, he wrote: "I always thought your writing at the *Village Voice* was overrated." I didn't respond. I mean, what can you say to that? But the thing is, his remark went into me. I'm a few months short of my sixtieth birthday, riding in a taxi to an artists' residency in Nebraska City. The driver is detailing his gastric bypass surgery and pointing out the hospital where it was performed. I'm in a taxi from

Omaha, because there is no public transportation to Nebraska City, and when we pull into town, I see why. The main street looks like a mouth with missing teeth, stores framing in their windows clues to their tragic abandonments: books scattered on the floor with their spines broken, apples rotting on a table under an inch of dust, chairs overturned like beetles on their backs. It looks like me, I think, this place.

Gertrude Stein, when she didn't know if she had anything to say, before she concocted the pellucid but indecipherable style that gave away nothing as it gazed with seeming serenity at everything, before she invented herself as a fat Buddha, devised a system to divide people into two categories. You could divide anything into halves, like loaves of the brain. Stein's idea was derived from her study of psychology with William James, before she dropped out of medical school saying, "You don't know what boredom is." She thought there were people whose natural way of fighting is the attack and people whose natural way of fighting is resistance. As soon as I read this, I thought: Toby and I, attack; Ellen and my father, resistance. My sister says she was subsumed by Toby while I escaped. She says, "You got the better deal." "Yeah," I respond, "but you got the diamond."

During my mother's last months, she sits with her eyes closed, her hand propping her chin. "It's as if she's going to sleep, but she's thinking," Ellen says, "waiting for death."

In December, Toby asks Ellen, "When is Laurie coming?"

"In a week."

"Then I'll have both my daughters with me."

Whatever she wants, I think, what can it hurt?

After she dies, I see her inside a chicken instead of a gizzard, a heart, and a liver. She used to chop chicken in a wooden bowl, along with green pepper, god knows why, and lace it with mayonnaise from the health-food store, and she said to me on more than one occasion but not often that I should have it, and I've got to tell you it was tasty. I slip slivers of garlic into chicken flesh I stab, opening little mouths and the memory of the knife when her chest was slit and wouldn't heal and she pointed to the stitched red gash with a cock-eyed grin and said, "Like a chicken." "Like a chicken," I agreed. She once typed a paper for me in high school, and as she unscrolled the first page we noticed bits of chicken stuck to it. "They must have fallen into the roller," she said.

In the 1970s, my sister's husband buys a health-food store on Fifty-second Street, and my parents work there, my mother in the front, the Czarina of vitamins, my father, the ex-coat manufacturer, in the back, whipping up smoothies and lunch specials. "Where is Toby?" people ask first thing. My mother is never happier; the streets are inside the shop. She kibitzes with Greta Garbo, pretending not to recognize her. "You, Toby," Greta asks, "you know what it is, a man?" My mother shoots a look at Murray, who is slicing an avocado. "That's what I know, end of story." The store booms for ten years, but the landlord jacks the rent and Mark is forced to sell. After my father dies, my mother cooks for God's Love We Deliver, an organization that feeds homebound people with AIDS. She stands on her feet during three-hour shifts, dicing onions, potatoes, and carrots. She's part of a crowd again, and they drag her out for coffee and Chinese food. God's Love is what she talks about: Karen's dating debacles, Ben's heart murmur. I volunteer there, too, and one day the head chef calls me complaining that Toby is making racist remarks. They've put up with it for more than a year. "Talk to her," he says, and so I go to her apartment and we sit at the cherry-wood table with walnut inlays.

"May I be struck by lightning if I ever said such a thing." She doesn't look me in the eye. "They're lying."

"Frankie says you talk about 'them,' use the word 'swartzers'. Everyone knows what that means."

"You're siding with strangers?" She shakes her head and presses her lips together. "I should have known you'd sell me down the river."

"I'm on your side," I say, but can this be true? She wants my allegiance no matter what. I want hers. What else is new?

She eyes a plaque on the wall: a reproduction of an Assyrian lion hunt from the Met. A lion is crouching at the feet of galloping horses, mighty in himself with eyes ablaze but cornered. "Who the hell are they to tell me what I can and cannot say? What, I'm going to be fired from a volunteer job?"

"How would you feel if people slammed Jews?"

"They hate Jews! That's why they're ganging up on me."

"Ma, you're doing the same thing."

"People are jealous of Jews. Blacks deserve what they get."

"*All* black people?"

"No. Some, I like."

"Well. You have to think about other people's feelings."

She sets her cup down hard, and the saucer rattles. "I thought about other people my whole life. I don't want to be gagged."

"Just stop being nasty. How hard is that?" What am I talking about? I wake up mornings with lists of friends I've offended and lost. The rats that survive the longest are the ones that adapt. The rats with the longest lives cart around the fewest unhappy memories.

Toby is silent, searching for a way to be herself and still remain at the party. In the end, she's asked to leave. She looks sad and ashamed when she tells me, and I feel for her, but then blood flows into her cheeks. "I don't need them. I don't need to work there anymore."

During the months before she dies, she goes in and out of dementia. When her aides go shopping, she flings herself from her wheelchair onto the floor and tumbles to the door, bringing down tables and chairs. She can't walk, but there is strength in her right hand and leg. She strips off her pants and underwear, crawls into the hall naked, and bangs on neighbors' doors. She wheels herself to the elevator, rides to the lobby, and tells the doormen she's being beaten by her aides. She wants contact. Every time she falls, she has to be picked up and held. Before she's disabled, she's uncomfortable with touch. Afterward, she kisses people's hands and slides them across her cheeks. She is scared that Primrose, who has been with her since she returned from rehab, will leave. I say she won't.

My sister tells a story. My mother is having coffee after attending a class at Hunter College, when a voice burns through the cafeteria din, "So you're still alive." It's my mother's sister, Etta, who disappears again, or maybe Toby lowers her head. Next a card arrives in the mail with a picture of a snake on it, signed Etta. "You believe this happened?" I ask Ellen. My mother's address and phone number are unlisted.

One time when Ellen calls Toby, Prim asks my mother if she knows who Ellen is. Toby says, "My sister." I think she may have confused Ellen's name with Etta's, or mixed up the words *daughter* and *sister*. When Ellen visits, Toby remembers a quarrel with Etta, and Ellen says, "She's probably dead." Toby bursts into tears, saying she has seen her sister on TV, waving to her.

On the phone, my mother tells me: "Primrose says you come to New York every week and don't visit." It's not true, I say.

"That's what Primrose says."

My mother reminds me of my grandmother when she was old and confused. She once called me to report she'd read Toby's obituary in the newspaper and wanted to know where her daughter was buried. Did she want Toby dead, given that my mother had refused to speak to her for more than ten years?

On the phone, Toby asks if I have children.

"No."

"Why not?"

"They're not that easy to produce."

"I thought you would have six by now."

I look at my hands that are hers, small boned and veiny.

I am pushing Toby's wheelchair up the hill on Fifty-seventh Street. She is nearing ninety-two. Primrose walks beside her.

"Toothpaste, cotton swabs, witch hazel," my mother says, fists waving. She is bundled in a wool coat and a fake fur hat that frames her pretty, hollowed face.

"You told me twenty times." Prim's jaw is clenched, her eyebrows to the roof. Prim is what separates my mother from a nursing home. She's wearing a navy parka and a wool hat pulled low over red dreadlock extensions. My mother absently holds a glove, and Prim pockets it.

I ask my mother if she's happy to be out.

"How can I be happy?" she says in a reedy voice, a question she might have posed at any time in her life. I see more strain than usual beneath the dimples that etch her cheeks—a smeared, blitzed look, like one of those murdered or murderous faces painted by Francis Bacon.

"Don't give up your apartment," she says, as we wait for a light on Columbus Circle. "Don't be stupid."

Cars whiz close to the curb. The glass of the Time Warner Center—New York City's first enclosed shopping mall with posh restaurants and shops—rises impassively over the empty fountain surrounding a statue of the Italian mariner. It's as if he's come all this way to be in the center of the world, the New York everyone noses to and feels shipwrecked from if they have to leave. When Richard lived here, he thrived among people who were charmed by rather than snooty about his non-Oxbridge vowels—*toof* for *tough* and *soofer* for *suffer*. Two mounted police patrol the gate of the park. Vendors sell souvenirs and framed photographs, including the famous shot of John Lennon with his round specs and shoulder-length mane, perched on a ledge on the Upper West Side. Richard and I have talked about coming back. My place could be a base, although it's too small to stay in for long and he needs the right job. It is a law of the universe—as firm as the principle that mass and energy are interchangeable—that you don't give up a rent-stabilized apartment in New York. You maintain your resident status, holding a chair against landlords who want to slash your throat so they can triple the rent.

I seem not to care. I am floating, blimplike, over my past, all of which—my early years in Washington Heights, my student days at Barnard and Columbia, my long tenure at the *Village Voice*, my love relationships and passionate friendships—have been tangled in the spaghetti streets of the city. It's so much my medium, I can't feel it. I mean, does a fish know it's swimming in water?

At Columbus Circle, it doesn't cross my mind that when my mother speaks about my apartment she is thinking about *hers*—fearing her aides will leave, worn out by her, and that she'll be exiled from the only existence that breathes life into her and that she contributes to with her huffing theatrics, my mother the character, my mother with a role in the only show she wants to attend. Even in her wheel-chair, she buses to Fairway, searching for a nectarine that won't break her heart. I say her aides won't leave, but it makes no impression. I don't consider she's worried about me. I can't hear her, can't hear my friends who say, "Don't lose your bearings. Don't lose yourself." I think they're saying, "You can't have love. You can't have happiness." They say: Look before you leap, but the horizon looks like Richard.

"Laurie's not going to give up her apartment," Primrose says. She turns to me. "I tell her the same thing every day."

The sky is gray and pillowy, and a light rain falls; Toby doesn't notice. A police horse walks close and its wet hair scents the air. It snorts, and my mother jumps. "I'm afraid of horses. I'm afraid of everything. Laurie, don't let the horse get so close. It will step on me. It will bite me."

"More likely you'll bite the horse," Prim says, eyeing Toby with the affection of their early days, her mouth swerving to the side. She's played reggae for Toby and danced, my mother exclaiming how talented she is, how sexy. They talk about sex, Prim lying beside Toby on her bed. Toby is curious but says she was afraid of sex, too. For a moment Prim is Island Girl again, her hips swaying and her laugh full-throated, the beauty from St. Ann's and later Kingston who walked through fields of ginger and annatto, a gorgeous woman pursued by men who married one, only to cut him loose when he proved more an anchor than a float. She has made me swear not to tell Toby about the new man she's seeing, fearing that my mother will tear him down.

"Me bite a horse? I don't even like horses."

"You don't like anything. You don't need anything, do you, Toby?" Prim says.

"That's right. I wish I could live by myself."

The light changes, and we cross. A pack of teenagers with a rain-bow of skin colors lopes by, behind them an elderly couple navigate by themselves. Two Wall Street types in long coats and leather boots bound up from the subway, jog to make the light, then disappear into the Time Warner Center. A bus wheezes to a halt and coughs out sundry denizens, some heading for the shops, others for Eighth Avenue. My mother regards them enviously. On the other side, I press down on her wheelchair, and she swings back like a patient in a dentist's chair.

"Why are you going to Arizona?"

"To be with Richard." I hoist her up to the curb.

"Do you pay for the plane tickets?"

"Yes."

"Why?"

"I want to be with him."

"I wish I had your money." She chuckles and twists her head. "Why are you giving up your apartment?"

"I'm not."

"You said you were giving up your apartment."

"I didn't."

"You don't know how things will turn out. Where will you go? Don't be a fool. No one gives up an apartment in New York. Why doesn't he come to you?"

"He has a job."

She turns her face to the side as we make our way through the glass doors, and I wheel her across the marble rotunda. Her profile is still beautiful. Her cheekbones jut glamorously. "He's a poor slob," she says in a dreamy, Mad Hatter voice, addressing the air more than me.

Eight weeks before my mother dies, she's admitted to the hospital with mysterious bleeding. Bladder cancer is suspected, but I don't believe she has it. I think she'll return to her apartment and that I'll see her again. I think she'll meet Richard, even if she has no idea who we are. It turns out she doesn't have cancer. She dies in her bed, approaching ninety-three.

"She's gone," Ellen says on the phone, driving to Toby's apartment. After my mother's stroke, she learned she had fibrosis of the lung, which is incurable and untreatable. It was supposed to have killed her a long time ago, and finally it did. According to the coroner, she suffocated in her own fluids.

Richard speaks about two types of museums. The kind like Noah's ark that aim to exhibit samples of everything that exists, such as the

Museum of Natural History in New York. And memory palaces: idiosyncratic collections, commemorating local history you find in any small town.

I sleep in Toby's bed, organizing her things. When Ellen and I learn that her furniture has value—a lamp, for instance, is the work of the Italian designer Gino Sarfatti—I vote to auction it, including a small table I've thought of keeping. I prefer my capital liquid. Toby wore a deco diamond ring on her left pinky I would follow as her hand swept this way and that. "You'll have it when I'm dead," she would say, smiling, unable to imagine her extinction, same as everybody. I didn't understand why she was wearing it in the hospital. I thought it might be giving her comfort, and I didn't remove it for safe keeping. When it was stolen, I felt the ground tilt as I do as I write, still falling for the same old con.

I make my way through Toby's freezer, cooking pieces of chicken bent like arthritic fingers. I pack up a set of black, silver-rimmed plates, service for twelve, never used. Outside, my mother skitters along Fifty-eighth Street, stands in front of the Plaza Hotel on the red carpet secured with brass rivets, chats with the doorman while scanning the distance for the dot that is me. Maybe I've been abducted by aliens! I should be so lucky.

My mother wouldn't have cared about the garbage bags stuffed with her clothes, still in plastic from the cleaners though some with stains, and her chipped, everyday plates with the autumn-leaf design worn faint. I throw away a dozen pairs of Easy Spirit shoes, character style, with a strap across the instep. I see her at the dining table with the harlequin inlays, above her a modernist chandelier, a burst of twelve tulip fixtures selected by Julie Stein, the interior decorator she trotted behind in the late 1950s when our summer cottage was converted into an all-year-round house. Toby is hunched over a book that rests on a stand, a conservative talk show blasting on the radio.

Eight months before she dies, she's admitted to St. Luke's Hospital after a psychiatrist deems her in crisis. The aim is to get her started on a new mood stabilizer—the previous ones having failed. My sister is fed up with Toby, who is screaming pretty much all the time. Ellen is disowning her mother with the freedom of the loved child. But

Toby touches me and reminds me of Al Swearingen, the sympathetic monster at the center of the HBO series *Deadwood*, who also reminds me of myself. Played by British actor Ian McShane, his dark eyes ringed with pain, he is always stealing himself for the next brutality he is going to unleash on the world, as if his savagery is against his will, as if his cruelty is a tyrant driving the obliging but reluctant servant that is also him to carry out his deeds.

I call my mother on her ninety-second birthday, and she sounds groggy but there. "I disappointed you by not giving you money and by calling Richard 'a poor slob.'"

"Why did you say that?"

"I didn't mean anything. I say the same things about Mark."

"You've known Mark for forty years. You've never even met Richard."

"Yes, you're right."

She is seeing herself more clearly, even as she slips away. She's sorry about the money but still doesn't offer me any.

In Arizona, Richard and I stand on our patio and watch lightning fracture the black sky. Pollack flings of furious beauty skip across the night, and the darkness shudders like a body waking from the dead. I squeal with each illumination, night becoming day in a confusion of the natural order. "Everything gets rubbed," Richard says, looking up at the crackling night.

I propose we write about the concept of the muse, a marble of a thought that's been tumbling in my head. A professor friend of mine has been teaching my work and has referred to Toby as my muse. At first I shove the idea away, but then I see that every piece I write about longing—and isn't everything we write about love or something hurting what we love?—starts with an ache for my mother. It has the shape of shadow moving over desert mountains, across giant saguaro cacti with their arms outstretched, across higgeldy-piggeldy rocks, some red colored, some blackened and inscribed. It is a blank sky— like a brain before it's marked with impressions.

At the start of a hike, I stand on the road while Richard studies trail maps. He explains where we are going, but I don't care. I know the walk will be arduous and hot and that I will not exactly enjoy it, rather want to go along and hope to see lizards and birds. Hikers share trails with mountain bikers. What they do—bobbling up crazily steep paths and hurtling down the other side—looks torturous. It's the ordeal you choose rather than passively endure—the dare that feels like a right to exist.

Shade is beautiful in the desert, cutting a knife edge against glaring light, bleeding across wide, vacant space. One day, we arrive at the top of a hill, and Richard sees a still higher point crowned by black, jutting rocks. As we scurry up, we realize we've come to the old wall of a fortified area. A small sign indicates an archaeological site, but it isn't marked to attract visitors. Around us are hundreds of petroglyphs: designs scraped out on desert varnish by people who lived in the region nine hundred years ago. All traces of them have vanished except for this graffiti. I copy a design into my notebook that looks like a Giacometti figure, a pared down, twig thing—a remnant of ourselves we carry inside.

When I think about New York, I see my mother's feet stretching down to the Lower East Side, her fingers up to Carnegie Hall. She dreams of her legs running for a bus. "I'm not young anymore," she says to the man with a mustache who guides her up the steps. "I wish I had your youth, darling. I wish you good health, you are so kind." I see my mother on her bed, pulled behind a boat. She is flying across waves and she is afraid, but that is the element she remembers as her music. Even as a young girl, her eyebrows knit as if seeking each other in consolation. We don't know who we are. It isn't a human capacity, so you might as well wish for a golden beak to sprout from the parrot colored feathers on your face. I'm sorry for your loss, people say, but what is my loss? I'm glad I'll never see her again. I wish she were alive.

# Cardinal

Ben Nachumi

So lately we have come along

hoping to understand this
multitude of whistling tongues

to decode in cackles
the frankness of grackles

the subtly mock-hymnal
sobbings of doves

Sure it's song, but to what use?
Love's inflection? Bright abuse?

Cordial in the gloam, one lights
quips his quips and flits: it's night

# Apnea

Have you ever
as the dreamer
as the salmon
in its stream
dreamed you dreamt
another dream, so caught
a second in its net
gasped, fishmouthed

to breathe air again
self-rescued with
a timely twitch
the thought that *that*
was just a dream, that
since you are endowed
with lungs, respiration
is allowed, and swum
through to the next episode

Exhausting sport
this layered
extreme sleep
Morning reaches
your head
inert, artifactual
coconut in a soft
impaction of pillows

Ben Nachumi

# Advice

As you quest for audiovisual companionship
Prudence is truth
You don't really need the big one

All those extras, but for ten times
The *tsuris* of your basic set
All I'm saying is
Don't be seduced by what is "best"
An imperfect image can be more than good
Enough for private pornography
In a dark apartment

You already know what you like—
We men are hard-wired
And lack only the suggestion
Of a proximate form
To buy the story of desire

# The Wedding Men

Now come boating
On big shoes, the long
Shanked, belted ones

Not all of them handsome
Some, their heads bewildered
Passengers on their shoulders

Our best is done to chase
Bad luck; we speechify
Fumigate the place with cigars

In standing for the toast
Our chair legs make
A chorus of trombones

# The Pride of Life

## Christopher Sorrentino

TOLLER'S MOTHER WITHDREW FROM THE WORLD AT THE AGE OF forty-five, when Toller's parents moved to California after Toller's father accepted a job with a computer company in Santa Clara. Toller's mother instantly found the region to be uncongenial, and retired to her bedroom, where she would stay, more or less, for the next twenty years. Toller himself was young then, in the pride of life, and to the extent that he was aware at all of his mother's reclusiveness he assumed that since she was now old, she had every reason to stop being an active participant in life. Toller's father was absorbed in his work and either paid little attention to his wife's increasingly eccentric behavior or did not confide in his son about his concerns.

After Toller graduated from college, he and the girlfriend he'd had since his sophomore year broke up and Toller decided to follow his parents to California, having heard, as everyone used to hear, about how inexpensive and easygoing it was in the Bay Area.

"Great," his father said. "Can't wait to be able to see you all the time, sport."

"Oh, Toller," his mother said, "why would you want to come to this miserable place?"

Toller came anyway, bouncing around for his first few months before settling in the East Bay, in Rockridge, where he took a room in a big house on Bryant Avenue he shared with four other people. Once a month or so he borrowed a car from a friend and drove to Palo Alto to visit his parents at their small house in College Terrace. His mother would come out of the bedroom, and the two of them would usually spend some time sitting alone on the patio in the backyard, a quiet little space that caught the breeze and was shaded by a mature cotoneaster and a lemon tree. Richly colored bougainvillea climbed over the fence and up the rear of the house. His mother had hung a hummingbird feeder from the kitchen window overlooking the patio and often one of the creatures would buzz past them to feed. Toller would watch the blur of the bird's wings as it hovered, dipping its beak into the feeder's fuchsia-shaped port.

"There he is," Toller's mother would say, "my best friend."

"Wow, he's really great," Toller would say, admiring the bird's ruby throat and precise, almost mechanical, movements.

"My best friend out here," his mother would repeat.

Toller would find this sort of exchange disconcerting: he'd bargained on admiring a bird (or a pretty house nearby, or the smell of eucalyptus, or whatever seemingly innocuous subject had briefly shuffled into position before them), and now he felt obliged to console his inconsolable mother in her loneliness. She would explain to him, again, that it was impossible here: no one interesting to talk to, nothing interesting to do, and nowhere interesting to go; and although Toller found none of these things to be true, at twenty-three he wasn't yet prepared to reject sweeping, categorical generalizations, least of all when they came from his mother. In any case there was little to do other than to agree with her, since she seemed to grow irritated with him if he did otherwise.

Things happened to Toller over the next few years—he grew close to some people and drifted away from others; he took jobs that interested him, that bored him, that paid well or poorly; he traveled, he enrolled in courses, he moved to San Francisco with a friend, he played in a band. He took advantage of some opportunities and missed out on others. He was an ordinary person whose life began to take on a reliable shape, and when he took stock of his small share of failures he did not, as a rule, have regrets, or anyway he didn't dwell on them.

Throughout, he returned again and again to the patio. The plastic hummingbird feeder grew cloudy and opaque and his mother replaced it. If it was rainy or cold, he and his mother would sit in the wing chairs adjacent to the fireplace in the living room. They'd talk while waiting for Toller's father to arrive. His mother hated the weather and felt that it was making her sick. His mother, who refused to learn to drive, hated having to wait to be driven everyplace. His mother hated the shape in which sticks of butter were manufactured on the west coast, and she hated the taste of the milk. Since it had been some time since Toller's father had tried to persuade her to accompany him to the various parties, dinners, barbecues, banquets, and other functions that he liked or felt obliged to attend, she no longer talked too much about how she hated the people who were being presented to her as potential friends. She did, however, forge intense, empty attachments to supermarket clerks, pharmacists, medical technicians, hair cutters, and tradesmen who came to the house to make repairs, and though she knew nothing more about them than the things she learned making small talk, she would relate the information to Toller in minute detail. His mother would tell him the elaborate plots of the television shows she watched. If Toller told her about the things that were happening to him, she would grow silent, as if he'd rudely brought up an awkward subject.

When Toller was thirty, various circumstances coalesced so that he found himself, all at once, without friends, single, unemployed, and quite unhappy. Now, abruptly, he was receptive to his mother's particular view of things. For six months he sat on the patio or in the wing chair once and sometimes even twice a week, immersing himself in his mother's opinions. He felt, rightly, that they were closer than they'd ever been before. It was her invigorating sense of futility that helped him get past the difficulties of the period, that and the cash subsidies that his parents pressed on him. Eventually, he found a place to live that he could afford, he found a new job, he made new friends, he met a girl. Things eased; life began to regain its reliable shape, and for the first time Toller began to resist his mother's judgments, as though his fleeting keen appetite for them was overly reminiscent of the circumstances that had stimulated it. Besides, now that things had turned out well, so well, they seemed slightly ridiculous.

His new girlfriend, Margaret, was a lively and sensible young woman to whom a life like the one Toller's mother was living was incomprehensible, and she bluntly pointed out to him that it was more than merely *odd*, the apologetic word Toller had taken to using to describe his mother, but: pathetic, limiting, pathological, antisocial, paranoid, and crazy. She'd majored in East Asian studies at Stanford and Toller—who was both offended by this evaluation and strongly enough infatuated with Margaret to lend credence to her every utterance—pedantically questioned her qualification to make such a diagnosis.

"It's not a diagnosis, Toller. These are colloquial expressions in everyday use. When someone tells someone else that a third person they both know is paranoid or antisocial everyone's clear on the meaning."

They'd left the house in College Terrace and were stopped at a light on Page Mill Road. Glass office buildings sat facing the road from the south behind acres of parking and a wide strip of landscaping that ran parallel to the sidewalk; on the north side, hidden behind thick growths of trees, were the winding, circular residential streets nestled at the base of the Stanford foothills. Though it was a cool night, they had the windows partly open and the good smell of wood smoke came into the car.

"I'm not clear on it, Margaret."

"Wind chimes."

His parents' new neighbors were a couple around Toller's age who had moved into the house next door earlier that year; they had installed in their backyard a set of wind chimes whose presence, Toller had noted, was gradually unhinging his mother, who now seemed to view wind chimes as a prominent element in an imagined version of the loathsome state's coat of arms. For several months, no conversation with her had been without its obligatory reference to the ubiquitous device, whose percussive tones—when he'd even noticed them—Toller had always found pleasant. Tonight, Toller's mother had subjected them to an extended harangue about the neighbors' chimes: how the slightest stirring of the air caused them to jangle, how their particular pitch was especially annoying and atonal, how the breeze itself—once so welcome and refreshing— seemed to be conspiring against her, invariably starting up at exactly the moment when she sought out a quiet moment on the patio . . .

Margaret had interrupted: "Have you talked to the neighbors? Maybe they'd be willing to move the chimes, or even take them down."

Toller's mother waved the idea away irritably, her lips pursed. "I've never spoken to those people," she'd said.

Now the light turned green and Margaret put the car into gear. "That was really something," she said, softly.

"Yeah," Toller said. "She's odd. I agree. But it's been hard on her out here. Totally new place, no friends."

"Toller, she's made it hard on herself. She's made it impossible. How long has she been out here? Twelve years?"

"About."

"Does she even go to the movies?"

"She can't. She doesn't drive."

"Toller. My grandmother drives. She's eighty-two. Born and raised in Taishan. She learned when my dad finally persuaded her to move down to Campbell from the city."

Toller didn't know how to respond to the news of this awesome accomplishment.

"And friends, Toller? Doesn't she have any old friends she stays in touch with?"

Toller explained that his mother had perfectly naturally lost touch with some friends, had fallen out with a few others, and so forth. He did not mention the occasion, a year or so earlier, when an old family friend had called to say that she was traveling in the Bay Area and that she'd love to drop by for drinks one evening. Toller had been there on the evening in question, and was disturbed that his mother pulled the curtains and left the lights off when it began to grow dark. When the doorbell finally rang, at about six o'clock, his mother had raised a hand for silence, and the three of them had sat there in the dark, his mother with her index finger laid across her lips, until the intruder had departed.

"Let's assume for the sake of argument that she's right," Margaret continued. "That it's horrible here: horrible, vapid, unwelcoming. Which isn't true, Toller. You know it isn't. I'm from here. It's very hard for me to sit across that table from her and politely listen while she tells me that everything I identify with is stupid and phony. And also when you agree with her, which, really. But let's assume just for the sake of argument that she's right. How often does she leave?"

"Leave?"

"You know. Get on a plane and go back to whatever home means to her. Take off for a week in Rome or Paris. Hawaii. She doesn't work. Your dad makes money. How often does she get away from this horrible place?"

Toller remained silent, half-expecting to hear about the heroic grandmother's annual pilgrimages back to Taishan.

"You're the one who told me that your mother never leaves the bedroom. What is she, a character from a nineteenth-century novel? Some Victorian lady with the vapors? What is that if not antisocial, and pathetic?"

"I wouldn't have told you if I knew you were going to use it against her."

"First of all, reminding you of something that you yourself told me is not using it against her. Second of all, you wouldn't have had to tell me a thing."

Margaret was right, but for now Toller only amended his thoughts of his *odd* mother to characterize her as someone who'd *lost her way*. That her actual life, a life that held her interest, had always seemed to exist at some point in time prior to the present, that the possibility of fulfillment had always seemed irretrievably lost to her, were conclusions that eluded him, as if the long crisis and profound isolation of the current setting threw these essential truths into such sharp relief that they were unrecognizable. Margaret was right, and for love of her Toller did find the limit to which he was willing to subjugate himself in order to align his behavior with his mother's expectations, as always defined by her cloistered outlook. Margaret was right, and she alone seemed to have established a rapport with Toller's mother, a rapport she felt she'd achieved through the respectful exercise of candor. She thought the older woman needed to be stood up to; needed— to use another colloquial expression in everyday use—a reality check. But Toller's mother's refusal to accept her adult son's assertion of his adult prerogatives was beyond Margaret's understanding, and she couldn't imagine how reckless nearly everything that he undertook seemed from the vantage of the bedroom. So when Margaret was seven months pregnant with Toller's baby and the couple decided to take advantage of their underemployment to spend two weeks alone at her parents' cabin on the north shore of Lake Tahoe, Margaret urged Toller to assert himself while he nervously prepared to inform his parents over the phone of their plans. She didn't understand his nervousness. He was thirty-two.

"Why would you want to go there?"

"It's beautiful, Mom."

"Toller, nothing in California is beautiful. It's all ugly. And you sound like a jackass, a true California jackass. One of those jackasses who's always talking about *getting away*, about *taking the weekend.* One of those sun fetishists who worships the weather and the fresh air. One of those self-righteous jackasses who belongs to hiking clubs, who wears a baseball cap, who—"

"Mom, we're going. Margaret really wants to take this time before the baby comes."

"And what about the baby? Don't you think you ought to be more careful about money, now that you're expecting a child?"

"I don't . . . I'm not . . . I—"

"How are you going to take care of it, hm? It's a big responsibility, a baby. Have you given it any thought? Any thought at all? Or is it all you and Margaret can do to think about your fun, your vacation at this lake? This is a life, a human life, that you are responsible for— forever! Neither of you has a real job. If I were in your shoes I'd just take those two weeks to hunker down with the classifieds each morning and try to find work. It's time to be an adult, Toller, not one of these jackasses here in California, grown men and women driving pickup trucks, who think life is all about fun and bicycling in silly shorts and a helmet and wind chimes. Wind chimes! For God's sake!"

Toller drew his attention from the abyss that had opened in the telephone receiver he held in his hand; looked around the apartment, that his mother had never seen, the apartment in which he and Margaret lived; at the books and pictures, the newspapers and mail stacked on the table, the stasis and the flux, at Margaret herself and her wondrously swollen belly, all the evidence of his life that his mother refused, at the risk of derangement, even to acknowledge. The fullness of it all, the friends she would never meet, the adventures she refused to take interest in, the enthusiasms she could not comprehend—even his own child, this grandchild, she would never really know; her stunted awareness would derive only from the monthly appearances it would make on the patio. Toller's mother should have understood him as well as anybody, but she understood only that he was the suddenly recalcitrant instantiation of the child who had once unquestioningly accepted her authority over every sphere of his life.

"Toller!" she brayed. "I don't want to hear about it if you find yourself in financial trouble! When you were coming down here a couple of years ago so upset and unhappy, I thought you were coming to your senses! But it appears that you're forgetting every lesson you should have learned!"

For the very first time Toller understood that his mother was truly the enemy of everything he was, all the things he'd sedulously worked to become, and that their connection had always been entirely, deceitfully, dependent on his successfully masking those things from her. Even her embrace of Margaret seemed doubtful: with the spat pronunciation of the hard consonants in words like *California* and *jackass*, words struck against the palate as if to generate sparks, he knew that she was identifying for him what she saw as the exact source of the contamination.

"Mom," he said, "I know what I'm doing. It's a vacation. People take them."

"*People*. Only in California would *people* take a vacation when they're not working! Vacation from *what*?"

"I don't have to ask your permission, Mom."

"How dare you!" she said. "How dare you! You little so-and-so!" There was a strangled noise, as if the heart of her indignation was beyond expression, and she slammed the phone down, leaving Toller, and Margaret, shaken.

Toller's father, vivid to him in nearly all other contexts, seemed to him (it must be said) to be a cipher in connection with his mother; Toller had no idea whether his father was concerned about his mother or not, whether he truly agreed with her condemnation of their lives or simply humored her, whether that placid agreeability masked a secret life of his own. Toller knew that his father got up and dressed and left the house every morning, that he came home every evening with stories of the greater world, that he sometimes met other people for lunch or golf, that he kept in touch with old friends. When he would join them on the patio, or by the fireplace, or around the dining table, he listened to Toller's mother attentively, although she could not possibly have been drawing anything new to complain about from within the enclosure of her life. His father's uncanny equilibrium was such that Toller had sometimes felt, before he met Margaret, that his mother's *oddness* was entirely a product of his own imagination. Perfect loyalty is what it was; Toller's father was loyal to a fault—but Toller wouldn't have understood this if he hadn't grasped, three weeks after their return from Tahoe and nearly six weeks since he'd spoken to either of his parents, the furtiveness of the call he received from his father one morning.

"Toller, you have to call your mother and apologize."

"Why do I have to apologize to her?"

"She feels very strongly that you spoke out of turn."

"And that's how you feel about it? Out of turn. She's the one who spoke out of turn. It was her. I can run my own life. I'm having a kid. I'm thirty-two years old."

"I know you are, Toller."

With each declaration of maturity, Toller felt more flustered and infantile. It went on like that for a few minutes. Toller wanted badly for his father to acknowledge that his mother had been wrong— wanted his father to acknowledge more than that, actually, although he was sensible enough not to share his developing opinions on his mother's mental condition—but the subject was taboo.

"How about her apologizing to me? Have you asked her that?" Toller asked again.

"I can't, Toller." His father was calling from his office, but he lowered his voice. And here Toller recognized the fragilely balanced forces holding together the marriage, and what must have seemed to his father to be his own life; his having reached, at sixty, the limits of its adaptability. Toller's father wasn't calling as his mother's envoy, or as Toller's ally, but as a man maneuvering to avoid a choice that would result either way in an unbearable loss. Toller understood; he hoped for the best with his mother, but he couldn't stand the idea of losing his father. He called and apologized.

Toller's mother continued scrupulously for a while to all but ignore Toller. It was so awkward, the way that she would talk around him if possible, as if he weren't there, or brusquely tell him that she would call his father to the phone if she happened to answer when Toller called, that Toller half-expected her to stop the discomfiting game; to ask him if she had demonstrated to his complete satisfaction that—as with her other feats of self-estrangement—she was fully capable of sustaining this act of will: would he now conform to her requirements? For all that she required of him, she may as well have asked such a question of the entire despised state of California. Unexpectedly, she took to Margaret again wholeheartedly, which bothered Toller, who suspected that it was her coded way of denigrating the relationship; of subtly informing him that she saw a clear and definite separation between the two of them that she could emphasize by placing the wedge of herself in it, which seemed to be confirmed by Margaret's curious reciprocation of her evident affection.

"When a nasty old cat decides it loves only you, you always love it back," Margaret explained.

Margaret had attained the condition of hallowed and empty bonhomie embodied by the Safeway cashier, the phlebotomist, the man who sawed off the dead branches of the live oak in the front yard, all those *dear people* his mother thought so highly of. It didn't matter how or why. To remain in Toller's mother's good graces meant to have sustained the glow of some positive impression, no matter how arbitrarily it had been registered. The impression didn't need to have any depth. Toller's mother certainly didn't want to know any more about Margaret than she did about those cherished strangers of hers: she became visibly uncomfortable if Margaret spoke to her of her childhood in the South Bay; or of her father, a radiologist in San Jose, and her mother, the owner of a Hallmark store in Los Gatos. She did clap her hands with glee when Margaret told the story of her refusal to bend to her parents' will and follow a pre-med course at Stanford, but became perplexed and sullen when it was made clear that the resulting rift had been temporary and superficial, as if the deepest and most mysterious disappointment of the human psyche was the willingness to forgive other people. And when things finally eased between Toller and his mother, when she began again to speak to him as if he were more than an unwelcome stranger, it was plain to him that she had neither forgiven him nor stopped being disenchanted with him.

Toller might have wondered why he'd bothered apologizing at all; it was obvious that his mother suffered his presence only in order to see Margaret and the baby, a girl, who was—as Toller had predicted— delivered to the patio each month in the back of the late-model Toyota sedan that the new parents, having somehow avoided the financial ruin their vacation was sure to bring on, had bought used. He might have wondered if not for the fact that, as intended, his apology enabled him to continue to see and speak to his father—more so than before, even, since the job of sitting with his mother in the shade of the cotoneaster and the lemon tree now was delegated largely to Margaret and the baby, allowing Toller and his father to spend time together. His father was now partially retired, providing consulting services to his former employer for several well-compensated hours each week. Though Toller never pointedly inquired about his mother's habits, his father made it clear to him that the things he was doing in his now-abundant spare time he was doing by himself.

"And Mom?" Toller would ask, casually.

"Oh, you know your mother," his father would say. "She has her books and her cards and things. I just try to stay out of her hair."

Toller followed this obliquely delivered advice to the letter; he persisted in hoping for the best with his mother, but he had little idea what the best might be, and the degree of deformation inherent in the family mechanism became painfully evident on occasion, most notably when his mother refused outright to attend his wedding to Margaret and insisted that his father remain behind to chauffeur her to a scheduled doctor's appointment. Even the illusion he maintained of unfettered access to his father became strained to the breaking point in such instances, and in the case of their wedding Toller had to beg Margaret not to call his mother and give her a piece of her mind, fearing that if Margaret made it onto what they called his mother's "shit list"—this ordinary phrase evoked in Toller's imagination an actual lengthy document, with names inscribed indelibly upon it— he would never be able to see his father again.

Toller and Margaret continued to make their monthly pilgrimages to Palo Alto, eventually from the suburban town of Brisbane, where they moved into a house built on one of the lower slopes of a mountain. They raised their daughter, had another. Sometimes, in the evening, when he stepped out of the kitchen door and stood on the little redwood deck overlooking his backyard with a bottle of beer in his hand, watching his older daughter play in the soft light remaining with the sun now behind the mountain, listening to a mourning dove calling, that desolately beautiful sound he associated with the pale orange of twilight here, he'd think of the precipitating offense, of the misconception at its heart—wasn't this his house, his deck, his daughter, his beer? What had he done so badly? He was able to shrug it off, though: aside from the hunkering mystery of his mother, life was good to Toller, reliable and satisfying, and it was typical of a simplicity of mind that he would have been the last to suspect that he believed it would continue this way forever.

****

When Toller was forty-two, his father was diagnosed with a brain tumor, and he died six months later. Toller learned that his father was dead when his mother called while he was on his way to the hospital.

"Don't let them take him away," Toller said automatically. It was the most reflexive thing he had ever said, completely unprompted and unscripted, and he pondered it, this primal desire, as he drove along 280, exiting at Sand Hill Road and coasting down the long incline toward the Stanford campus and the medical center at its edge, Hoover Tower rising in the distance. A malfunctioning sprinkler operating on one of the emerald swaths of grass on either side of the road sprayed the windshield and passenger side windows of Toller's car as he passed, startling him from his reverie, and he fumbled for the wiper switch.

At first, after the diagnosis, Toller had been tremendously hopeful—hopeful that his father would survive, and hopeful that the crisis would repair the rift between his mother and him. Who else, he'd wondered, could she turn to? And who else, he might have wondered, did he have? Even a hated son resists the idea of his own orphaning. But although he'd carefully dressed and groomed himself for his appearances in his role as concerned adult son, hoping to gull his mother from behind the disguise of his ongoing success, she'd been unrelenting, and when Toller had checked the time on his wristwatch, a wristwatch he was proud of, as the two of them waited for his father to emerge from surgery, she had casually ridiculed it, gesturing at it as if to the very unseen audience to whom Toller was playing. "What kind of a watch is that? That's an absurd watch for a grown man." And, after the surgeon had finally appeared to deliver the unhopeful news, when Toller had leaned toward his mother and begun to say vaguely reassuring words, she had twisted the section of newspaper that she held in her hands—a section he had offered her in the courtly manner that he imagined was befitting a considerate and beloved son—into a club, as if she intended to strike Toller with it. His own newspaper!

"For God's sake, Toller. I don't need comforting. I don't need you to comfort me."

When he arrived at the hospital on the day his father died, he found his mother standing at the nurse's station, a paper grocery bag on the counter before her. He started for his father's room, but his mother's voice stopped him: "He's gone, Toller." He pushed through the voice; she couldn't possibly mean what she seemed to be saying, but when he reached the room it was empty, the bed already efficiently stripped.

"I wanted to see him," Toller said.

"You didn't want to see him like that."

"I *did*," Toller insisted. "I *did* want to see him."

"Well, I didn't want to wait in there with him while you took your time getting here," she said. "All right? Please, don't make a scene. If you want to see him, you can go down to the morgue. The morgue, right?"

A nurse looked up brightly from the computer terminal and open files before her and nodded. Toller's mother had one hand on her hip and rested an elbow on the counter. She looked as if she was at the front desk of a hotel, checking out. It dawned on him that in the grocery bag were his father's things. Toller sat down in a chair to wait while his mother squared things away. The chemo nurse came upstairs to hug her, the CT scan technician, the floor nurse, wearing a preposterous tunic depicting Sylvester and Tweety—stalking, chasing, pouncing, fluttering away, laughing. More of his mother's *great friends*.

Toller returned home to Brisbane that night—his mother having refused his perfunctory offer to stay with her at the house—and ate voraciously. He had his father's address book with him, and he wore his father's signet ring on his finger. The girls were in bed and Margaret sat across the kitchen table watching him. He ate what was before him and then returned to the stove to get more from the pot. He drank an entire bottle of wine. Margaret said nothing when he started on the whiskey. He felt elated. A feeling of well-being spread throughout his body, easing a knotty tautness that seemed to have entered deep into each of his muscles months and years beforehand. He wondered if this was what his father had felt as his own depleted body began its final shutting down, an easeful surrender of all the worst things life had thrust upon him. What, with that gone, would have been left to worry about? Surely he couldn't have been worried about that boulder of refusal, of imprudent harsh resolve, that turned up at the hospital each day disguised as a wife, disguised as a *person*, to stand at his bedside, imparting her spurious good cheer to the personnel who jabbed, who poked, who choked, who abraded, who tormented his father throughout those final weeks. That fantastic act, honed over the course of decades while the malignancy of her genuine feelings burned glowing within her, lavished upon those who professionally and without the least emotion presided over his father's destruction. After all that she could not forgive, all that fell short against that scale of rigid values she'd erected over the years, he found, with joy, that he could not forgive those smiles and tears she expended on them even after allowing their collaborators to haul his father away like meat. The two of them, mother and son, were free of one another at last. Thinking of his father dead—the imagined corpse that would always have to stand for the real one he hadn't seen—he began finally to cry for the first time that day, and Margaret reached out to take his hands in hers with the incomplete but heartfelt understanding that is the best, really, that we can hope for.

# "We're the bitches of the First World."

(Lipsyte, page 1)

# To Melancholy/Clear Windows

Dan Sofaer

I first encountered my ghost
At the corner of Twelfth Street
And Seventh Avenue, in the form of
A successful filmmaker.
I'd just gotten back
To the city of my birth
After constant travels.

(You know the way
When you step onto
Seventh Avenue it just seems
A sea of cars, and they
Don't have you the least bit in mind.
They have the Holland Tunnel in mind.)

She said, "Dead I still walk
Among the living. I even have
A job at the New School."

We walked together a certain distance.
At our outsetting, I listened to no music.
Clear windows shone opposite.

I said, ghost, does one always plunge back
Into the warm familiar songs,
Or is it important to travel
Whole continents?

She said, I cannot help you there.
My father owns a shipping company,
That has given me means.
Don't be afraid to be fanciful.
You'll find plenty of material here for dreams
And the photos of Nadar.

She was always silence,
Silence in music, and the familiar distant gods.

I called her later on the phone..
I said, the problem is, I
Learned the habits of solitude living abroad.
Only in these so-called New York diners
Do I feel adequately alone.

Why don't you feel alone at home? She asked.
My relatives! No sooner have we done with one visit than they begin
another. Tedium of family,
Blooming brides and so on.

She said, you're more of a ghost than I.
I still spend time with father among the dead.
I don't, I said.
Well, then, you've made your bed,
Or grave,
And now you'll have to lie in it.

# Stuck Speech

I lost my reason just like that,
Like an owl scared off by a cat,
But I gained:

Everything that ever happened when it rained.
Everything that ever happened in a car.
Till things started happening more in bars.
Chinatown, hot day in May.
Trucks cursed all in their way.

On a payphone, you saw a sign:
Ivolo, call me. Please
Don't take off this time,
Love is at stake.

# Blurred Inheritance

The inheritance of loving words
The mind's inheritances
Dreams, responsibilities (famously)
Are blurred now as
The rings of Saturn.

You can only have gotten ill somehow
Surely there must be some explanation?
You have forgotten our arrangements
As was clear at childish intersections
Where you refused to look out.

Often we have bent back our heads
Downwards and backwards to the sun
From swings at sunset bareheaded
And seen and explained to ourselves
A world upside-down.

# We Loved the World But Could Not Stay

## Gary Lippman

THOR YABOWITZ STOOD NAKED BEFORE HIS NEIGHBOR WHEN the "*bah-bah-bah*"s erupted from his cell phone. Each week he changed the ringtone to a different Beach Boys song, and "Barbara Ann" was loud enough for Thor to hear it from his kitchen.

"It figures," said Joni (whose middle name was Mitchell, courtesy of the hippie parents who were still together and retired in Scarsdale.)

"I'd, uh, better get it," said Thor.

She scowled at him. "I've only got, like, ten minutes!"

Ordinarily, on the cusp of clandestine quickie sex with his neighbor, or with *anyone*, he would have let a call go to voicemail. But today he figured that it might be Philomena, the actress he'd met three days before at The Bean that Rules Our Destiny Café. Was Philomena calling him back at last? If so, better to talk to her directly, not play another round of phone tag. Ignoring Joni's shout of "Don't you *dare*," Thor went sprinting on tingly bare feet from his bedroom to the kitchen, where he grabbed the phone from the counter while it still rang. An unfamiliar number blinked on its earwax-stained yet illuminated screen, area code 718: *Brooklyn?* And when the male voice at the other end asked for "Paul Yabowitz," Thor told it, "Speaking," because back then his name was still Paul.

"Mr. Yabowitz," said the caller, "I know it's the weekend, I hope I'm not disturbing you."

"Who's this?"

"Mr. Yabowitz, um, it's David Lang from Triton Genealogy. How are you, sir?"

"Fine," said Paul. He scratched his left cheek with a pinkie, thinking, *Wow, what a mistake.*

"Sir, we mailed you two charts recently, one tree for your maternal line, the, uh . . ."

"The Schaefers."

"Yes, and for your paternal line as well."

"I got them last week, thanks."

"You did? Terrific. Were you able to peruse them yet? Do you have any questions?"

*Perused.* Paul's Sunday afternoons were for chilling out, not fielding calls from genealogists. The sooner he got back to his Joni-quickie, the better. "To tell you the truth," he said, seasoning his voice with a dash of impatience, "I scanned them, but not in any detail. Why? And can't we discuss this some other time?"

"Of course, Mr. Yabowitz, of course. I just wanted to make sure that you're satisfied."

"Well, I am. Now if—"

"And, uh, incidentally," said David Lang, "I'm wondering if you happened to notice any…irregularities. Rather, any *regularities.*"

"Regularities."

"With the dates, yes."

Paul sighed, gazing through his grimy, not-cleaned-yet-this-millennium double-glazed living room windows at the darkening sky. From the bedroom came the sounds of his DVD player switching on and warming up. At least Joni was keeping occupied in his absence.

"Sorry, but what the *hell* are you talking about?"

"Well," said David Lang, "there was this matter that I noticed while reviewing your charts on Friday. Specifically, your paternal chart. Now, I don't think it's anything important, not at all—a minor matter, but . . ."

Because he cared little about whatever this clown Lang had to say, Paul's attention stayed fixed mostly on his bedroom, where Joni had started watching the jewel of Paul's porno collection, *Hamlet's*

*Swingin' Seventies: Get Thee to a Hot Tub!* Which was fitting, because Ophelia was portrayed by Paul's favorite red-haired porn siren, Barnetta Oak, whom Joni happened to somewhat resemble. And as husky-voiced Barnetta made saucy pre-coital conversation with her Hamlet—the hairless yet fortunately endowed actor Edwin Energizer—Paul's attention drifted to the framed vintage Beach Boys posters on the living room walls. From each poster, bearded Brian Wilson, the Boys' mentally troubled *wunderkind*, seemed to smile benevolently at Paul, who—prompted by Barnetta's first pleased groan—finally spoke up. He interrupted his caller's babbling with a brisk "Look, let's talk tomorrow. I mean, it's not a big deal, is it?"

"No, probably not," said David Lang. "Although my wife, she's superstitious, and she wanted me to call. Now, I mean. Still, we can discuss this business tomorrow . . ."

"Wait. Your *wife?* Why's your wife reading my family tree?"

"Oh, I'm *sorry*, sir—forgive me. It's just that I told her what I found . . ."

Paul's brow furrowed. The geneaologist finally had his full attention. "And what was it?"

"It would be easier if you had your paternal chart in front of you. Could you get it, please?"

And so, grumbling yet disquieted, the still stark-naked Paul Yabowitz padded into his study in search of that family tree. It took some rooting around before he found it. Then he brought it to his living room, where he dropped down onto the long American flag-draped couch and said, "Okay."

"Good," said David Lang. "Now please have a look at Chaim Yabowitz, your great-great-great-grandfather. Documentation for Eastern European Jews is sparse, so he's as far back as we could go. Do you see him on your chart?"

"Yup, at the top."

"And do you see the dates for Chaim's lifespan?"

"Born 1820 and died, uh, 1888."

"1888. So he lived into his late sixties. Now find *his* first-born."

"Easy. He's right there. Adam."

"And Adam's lifespan?"

"Adam Yabowitz, 1851 to 1900. Well?"

"As I said, sir, this is probably nothing, but…but stay with me on this, if you please, sir. Adam Yabowitz lived to the age of forty-nine."

From Paul's bedroom, Joni shouted, "Come on, you ditz!"

"One sec!"

On the DVD, Barnetta Oak's moaning and groaning kept growing stronger. As Paul remembered from previous viewings, she and her Hamlet were getting busy on a shag rug in a lava lamp-lit Elsinore *boudoir*. Could the caller hear it? *Actually*, thought Paul, *he's just a genealogist, so who cares?*

"Next comes Adam's son," the genealogist continued, "another Chaim: 1869 to 1907. Do you see him on the chart?"

Paul grunted his assent.

"And *his* son, 1902 to 1940, who is your grandfather, and then *his* son, Emmanuel…"

"What is this, a belated April Fool's stunt?"

"No, sir, I promise you."

"Well, there he is—Manny, my dad. Like his father, he died young."

"Precisely. According to the information you provided us for your chart, your father's dates are 1940 to 1978. So do you spot the recent pattern, Mr. Yabowitz?"

Paul chuckled. "There is none!"

"Actually, look again, please."

"Look at what, their names?"

"No—each man's age when he passed away."

"I don't see why—"

"Trust me. Please. Just do the math."

Which Paul did, twice, and finally he saw it, what this guy from Triton Genealogy was referring to: *Every first-born Yabowitz male since Paul's great-grandfather had died at thirty-eight years old. Not older, and not younger—thirty-eight.* The most recent dead Yabowitz, "Manny," had been driving home from work in a hard rain when his cherry-red Eldorado crashed on a bridge near Exit 18 on New Jersey's famous turnpike. At the time, Manny's son, his only child—Paul— had just turned six. Grown-up now, Paul was thirty-eight himself.

And because tonight was June 28 and his birthday was August 8, he had more than a month to go until he turned thirty-nine.

"Do you understand now why I'm calling, Mr. Yabowitz?"

After clearing his throat, which had gone dry, Paul said, "There's obviously just some error."

"You're almost surely right, yes."

"The dates, there must be something wrong. Have you checked them over? Like, *triple*-checked them?"

"I've checked the primary research more times than that, sir. My wife spent all day going over it with me. As I said, she's the one who insisted I call you. Twisted my arm, in fact. True, our sources could be erroneous—one slip of a pencil in city records, one year off in a birth or death could change it all. You know, break the pattern. Then again, clerks were careful about these things, and whatever supporting sources we turned up seem to confirm, well, all of it."

Radiating down from Paul's scalp to his lower back was an acute ice-cold sensation. Was this what people meant when they talk of chills running down their spine? Until tonight, Paul had assumed it was a mere figure of speech.

"Mr. Yabowitz?"

In the bedroom, Barnetta Oak was very loud, with her costar's pants and grunts making a counterpoint to her own. Paul cleared his throat again, the chills still rippling through him, up and down and all around. *This is like some bad dream,* Paul thought, *like a nightmare.* Answering his cellphone tonight had cast him into another dimension.

"Mr. Yabowitz?"

"I'm here," said Paul in a weak voice.

"Sir, as I said, I'm sure it's nothing…"

"So am I *cursed?*" Paul blurted. "Is that what you're saying, that I'm *cursed?*"

"Cursed? Oh *no*—in my opinion, it's most likely a quirk. A statistical, you know…a *blip*. Nothing to worry about."

"Then why are you calling me with it?"

"Well, to make a full disclosure. Just to make sure you're aware."

"Have you ever seen anything like this before, three men all dying at the same age?"

The geneaologist fell silent—which answered the question.

"And this isn't some sick *joke,* man?"

"I assure you, Mr. Yabowitz, I mean no harm. I wasn't sure until just now that I should even call!"

Paul's heart accelerated in his chest, its every two beats sounding like a *tick-tock*—like a time bomb. *This isn't happening*, Paul thought. *This is just a bad dream.* Still pressing the ear-waxy cellphone to his ear, he sank deeper into his couch, soaking the flag there with his sweat, while down the hallway in the bedroom, he could hear Barnetta climax, her piercing cry of "*Ai-yee-yawwww!*"—although this sounded not like joy. More like an old widow's lament.

# The flasher buys a painted turtle.

Adam Peterson

Her name is Rosy, but he never has to write the name so it might be Rosie. He tries to coax her toward him, cooing *Hello there. Hello there. We are in this together now*. The turtle is intractably alone. The flasher sads. Coos again, *I can see you. You're not so smart.*

# The flasher interviews for a job.

The interviewer leads him to an impossibly bright room. It's only her, him. She asks *Can I take your coat and hat?* He keeps them. *Where do you see yourself in five years?* He keeps that too. *What are your strengths?* He thinks about loosening the belt on his coat. *What are your weaknesses?*

# The flasher wakes.

Broken blind light glistens a lake of saliva and tears in the hand underneath his head. Sunglasses on, the brilliance is snuffed. Soon, the lake drowns in the bathtub where his trench coat billows as the cold water rises.

The Toby of Long Beach is backing up a finned, yellow Pontiac, looking over her shoulder with a cigarette twisted in her lips. We're headed to the Malibu Beach Club, and I am fat. (Stone, page 33)

# Where We Chose

## Sarah Malone

WE WERE THE THIRD OF EIGHT TOWNHOUSES IN BEIGE VINYL pressed into the shapes of boards, and red plastic shutters with no hinges, too narrow to fit the windows. Straw kept dust down on the lawns. Across the street, the earth from our foundations had been mounded to block our view of the tracks, and when trains passed the poplars and scrub maples half-buried in the orange clumped clay whipped and widened holes around themselves. Once an hour, bell dinging, an express sighed to a stop at the station up the road. That was why we had signed the lease: for an express to New York for Shawn and a good school district for Jacob.

In the evening while Jacob did homework and Shawn checked each channel's news I went out to get the mail. The sky was white and distant behind the cicadas and the scraping silhouettes of leaves. A streetlight lit the mailboxes and darkened the block beyond them. Mihaela, in Number Eight, was walking up from the corner. She was five foot three, with short, dark, curly hair and a tri-color Papillon at the end of a retractable leash. She'd been a pilot in the Israeli Air Force. Now she worked in the bond market.

She shook the leash. "If it wasn't for her, I'd be all ass."

"I know how that is," I said.

I worked from home, arranging my clients' words into brochures and annual reports: Copperplate for titles, Garamond for paragraphs;

*long-term appreciation* in bold, *may lose value* in thin letters at the bottom.

A tiny smile pushed up Mihaela's soap-translucent cheeks.

"So," she said, "you'll see lots of Olivia."

She waved a ghostly, waist-level goodnight. The Papillon bobbed after her into the last driveway before the pavement stopped and orange construction ribbons drooped between the trees. I stood until it was too dark to make out the forwarding labels on our mail—all bills. I felt the edges of the address windows, and the plastic rattling.

Olivia strode out the next day. Bugs and pollen were high on the four o'clock air. The sun was turning poplar tops to gold. I kicked the curb and Jacob ran Matchbox cars through the tip of our roof's shadow. He had Shawn's thick, mousy curls and my allergies, and tendency to sunburn.

"Those will have to be outdoor cars now," I said.

"I know," he said.

Olivia was top-heavy and dressed for it in Capri tights and an oversized pinstripe Oxford. She had blonde-streaked hair and over-sized sunglasses with plastic frames. Her son, Tanner, was eight. Olivia had been praying for a family with a boy his age.

"And here we are," I said.

"I know it's not that simple, but isn't it something, how you're here and we're here and the boys are the same age?"

"It is something."

She pointed to the townhouse between hers and ours. "They're moving out."

I'd seen them, the short man driving the tall man to the train, or maybe the other way around. I'd waved, and they'd smiled from their car.

"I guess they're a couple." Olivia's nostrils twitched like a rabbit's. She pushed her glasses up on her forehead and nodded at Jacob. "If you're thinking about football, Coach is the best in the district."

"Jacob is only in third grade," I said.

"Was he in regular school?" She nodded at Jacob.

"New York City public school," I said. "P.S. 199."

"Coach will be great for him." She squinted. The sun was full in her face and flashed on a small cross on a thin chain where her top buttons were undone. "Tanner started last fall and Coach has worked miracles."

"That's good." I meant to sound glad without agreeing about the miracles. Beyond the mounds, the rails were clicking. Jacob had worn six Matchbox lanes into the dirt and off the curb to the George Washington Bridge.

"Are you ready to go in and play blocks?" I said.

When Shawn got home, he would have to see the mousetrap I'd found in the lazy Susan, and the ant trap under the stove. The previous owners had said nothing about pests, but then we hadn't thought to ask.

School started the following week. For the first few days, Jacob and Tanner played trucks on the clay mounds when they got home. Tanner borrowed a Matchbox moving van that Shawn called Cabover Pete and Jacob had never liked. Tanner was thinner than I had pictured but his shoulders were already wide and they hollowed forward over his chest. In the morning, down where our street met the main road and the bus picked up the boys, Tanner lowered his head like a dog deciding whether to growl, attack, or cower.

One morning I asked him how he was.

"Fine." He squeezed out the f, top teeth sunk into his lower lip.

Jacob had run ahead of me to greet him. When the bus came, Jacob followed him to the back. As the bus pulled away I saw Jacob wave to me from a seat by himself toward the front. Walking back to the house, when I closed my eyes I felt my flip-flops slap against my heels and the warmth of my sunny cheek.

"You don't have to wait with them." Olivia was in a sport bra and yoga pants, pushing one of the supports of her porch railing.

"The main road is so busy," I said.

"Tanner waited by himself all last year. But that's okay." Olivia's voice rose at the end in a way that said it wasn't.

My face felt hot and my scalp itched off and on for the rest of the day. In bed, before turning off the light, Shawn said I shouldn't worry.

"During the week it's just Olivia and me," I said.

"I'm sorry you're stranded," he said.

"I'm not stranded."

"Well," he said, "you have to decide what's worth making an enemy over."

Headlights swept the ceiling. He liked the left side of the bed and slept best on his left side, facing out, even if it meant facing a wall.

In the morning, Jacob and I stood balancing where the curb curved out to the corner and crumbled to a stop. Tanner's thumbs were busy with a hand-held video game but he spared me two words: "fine" when I asked how he was, and "stuff" and when I asked what he was going to do in school that day.

It was a warm day and I worked with the upstairs curtains blowing in while leaves hissed and trains clattered to and from New York. Sixteen stopped and went before it was time to wait for Jacob. Walking down to the corner, I heard metal clang in one of the backyards, hand claps, a man's voice, and Olivia, amazed and yelling. Jacob got off the bus alone.

"Want to ride bikes?" I said. "Let's ride bikes."

We rode twice to the corner and back. Dump trucks shook the main road. I pointed to the logos on their hoods.

"Too fast," Jacob said.

"There were lots of trucks in New York," I said.

"They're bigger here."

"They're in a hurry," I said. "That's all."

He didn't want to finish the road without Tanner. I was sure Tanner wouldn't mind.

The man's voice called out again. Olivia's voice said, "Oh—you *have* to."

Mihaela was walking up the main road from the station. The man's voice said something and Mihaela waved in the direction of our backyards and nodded without stopping. She waved again when she saw me.

"Aren't you excited?" she said.

I took up her sarcasm. "Should I be?"

She explained: the moving truck was coming tomorrow for the men who were leaving, and the men had told us to take what we wanted of their perennials.

"I haven't even met them," I said.

"See what you're missing?" she said.

Olivia's garage door stuttered up.

"I wonder if she'll wave," Mihaela said. A black BMW SUV backed down Olivia's driveway and turned its brake lights to us.

"She must not see us," I said.

"I'm sure that's it," Mihaela said.

Most days were cold enough by then that I worked with shoes on and windows closed, and from indoors the trains sounded like only trains from their whistles. Once I went out on the back deck for air and heard Olivia's door slide shut. Squirrels were running through the woods. Branches creaked, and a highway sounded close and far away. A trowel handle stood in the grass below Olivia's deck. Marigolds with roots wound white around crumbled soil waited by neat holes in the turf.

It was easy enough to watch the mailboxes from my desk and go out for the mail when Olivia went out for hers. Someone with a red and blue elephant as a return address had sent her a large white envelope.

"I don't know what you want me to say," Olivia said. "You don't even wave."

"I haven't seen you."

"You know that you only wait for the bus because you want to." She stalked away. The breeze had made it under my top. I crouched at the mailbox and turned the key in its little lock until it stuck. The scooped-out clicks of her heels stopped at the far side of the street.

"Don't think it's not obvious," she said.

"I don't understand your problem."

"My problem? You are my problem."

The breeze pressed my top close, fluttered under its hem and shivered up my sides, and Olivia's door opened and slammed shut. The mailbox was empty and I was standing in the street while the wires undulated above the tracks. The undulation was imperceptible until you looked for it.

In the kitchen, the drip of the sink punctuated the hum of the refrigerator. I nudged the faucet into the one position that stopped the drip. The calendar over the sink had been Colorado aspens—yellow for September—for a month and a half. Each month was a different national park. Most I had never visited. I'd chosen the calendar so Shawn could see mountains. I lifted it from its nail and as I fumbled the edge of October sliced my finger. I gripped the last months of the year on both sides, ripped just below the fold and flung away the pieces. The loose ends floated to the floor. The previous nine months, being bound, got some momentum, knocked my water glass from the counter, and it shattered on the tile. Typical. At least my feet weren't bare. I buried the calendar in the recycling bin and got the dustpan and vacuum from the closet.

When I figured it was late enough for Mihaela to be home, I told Jacob not to answer the door, that Mommy needed to go up the street. I liked that: as if I went up the street often, and, as in New York, I might return with absolutely anything. My shadow slipped from the circle of our porch light, ran across five driveways to Mihaela's walk and shrank back to my feet as I rang the bell. Mihaela opened the door, eyes wide. "It's you."

"I meant to come sooner."

Her kitchen matched mine—oak cupboards, black appliances, bare wall where the calendar had been—but she had track lights and a high glass table with backless metal stools.

"Very New York," I said.

"I pretend." She perched cross-legged on a stool. She and her boyfriend had chosen the townhouse to be near his work. She'd taken over the lease when he moved to Las Vegas.

"Have you ever fought with Olivia?" I mimed a punch. "I mean, not really fought."

"Fought?" Her lips stayed slightly parted.

I shook in the small of my back while I explained. I tried tensing every muscle but my back would not stop shaking. Mihaela hopped from her stool.

"What we need is some wine." She pulled a bottle of Toscana from a rack in a bottom cupboard and looked at me, one eyebrow cocked. "Yes?"

"Yes." Jacob would be okay for one glass.

"It's my boyfriend's," Mihaela said. "My boyfriend's ex-wine. Did Olivia tell you she put statues of Saint Joseph under the guys' porch to get them to move?"

I told her about the football conversation, and about waiting for the bus. Later, I didn't like having used Olivia's words against her. I'd always been too busy for that kind of talk.

"After Olivia you have to talk out the crazy." Mihaela refilled my glass.

"That's it," I said. "I just needed to talk."

I was halfway through my third refill when my phone rang—Shawn.

"I didn't know where you could have gone without the car," he said.

"Not far," I said.

Shawn didn't notice where the calendar had been. We sat reading on the living room couch after Jacob was in bed, each of us at one end under a lamp.

"We should have Mihaela to dinner," I said.

"Sure," he said. "She seems like a nice girl."

"So what should I have said?" I drew up my knees and clasped my hands in front of them. "To Olivia."

Shawn had a shelf of books on managing difficult people. "The thing with negotiating." He put down his wine glass and crossed his legs. "You have to go into any conversation knowing what you want."

"We were just talking."

"Nothing is just talking. Someone always comes out boss."

"Is that how you think?"

"I try to."

"So, what are we doing now?"

"Listen," he said. "You wanted my opinion."

We read for a few more minutes and he said he was going up to bed. He was right, about conversations, though I did not tell him that I'd gotten exactly what I'd wanted from Olivia, or how Mihaela had understood.

"Now you can't be ambushed," she said.

She had grown up near a garrison on the Lebanese border. Rockets had fallen from hill towns that twinkled through the night air in the orange groves, and in restaurants and on buses anyone might have been readying themselves to detonate. She did not blame them.

"They look at my village and see tanks," she'd said. "So I came here, and I trade bonds."

"Lucky me," I said.

And I was.

# Congestion

## Michael McGrath

ON THE WAY HOME FROM WORK MY WINDOW IS ROLLED UP AND tinted. Everyone is going to the same small place. Make room. I can see the green sign indicating my exit through the late-afternoon glare. There is no movement in sight, just a frozen river of shiny-topped compacts with wisps of exhaust trembling upward. I pop mine into neutral and apply the parking brake. I have yet to fully learn how to make it through this daily ritual. It is too much time for me to safely spend alone. I see embarrassments in the rearview mirror. They are as close as they appear.

I would like a cleaner car. Often I wake up and tell myself that this is the day that I will hit the car wash. Sometimes I will even pluck quarters from my coin dish in preparation. But then it will rain, or I will have a particularly unremarkable day and I'll tell myself that I can't possibly endure one more mundane, upper-lower-middle-class task before crawling back into bed (not counting, of course, the glass(es) of buttery chardonnay, the Lean Cuisine(s), the dating Website(s)). Save the quarters for a blindingly sunny Saturday after an especially hearty Friday night. Save the quarters for a special occasion, like taking a girl out, driving home to see the folks, car-pooling with Greta from HR. Therefore the car stays dirty. Gets dirtier. Dirt accumulates.

After one dust storm, especially terrifying in its swiftness and efficiency, I almost couldn't find the car. It had disappeared into the side of the street along with everybody else's. As neighbors it was our duty to watch each other walk out of our homes and stagger up and down the street, pointing our keyless remotes every which way, begging for the relief of that *beep-beep*. When I finally found mine I almost kept walking. It looked like an ant hill. To climb inside it would mean something terrible. It would mean surrender: to the elements, to my neighbors, who all have nicer cars than I do. I live in a gated community, but I share the house with four other young men. Our patio furniture is mismatched and our decorating scheme is Staples casual: a leaning desk, a groaning book case.

I stood in front of my car and wrote in the dirt on the driver's-side window. I drew phalluses and enormous, lopsided breasts, as rudimentary as cave drawings. When I finally ducked in and turned the ignition, it sounded as if the dust had gotten inside the engine, flown up the exhaust pipe and infected every tube and piston. The whole thing felt gummy. I could, of course, see nothing in front of me. The windshield was coated. I applied the wipers, which seemed to only rearrange the dirt, somewhat artfully. I pressed the lever in, asking for washer fluid. It sputtered twice, ejaculating a pathetic amount onto the glass, where it congealed quickly into a small island of mud.

I had noticed over time that the stream of windshield-washing fluid was growing weaker and weaker. I even saw a jug of it at a gas station when I had gone in to use the restroom. I even checked the price of the jug and remarked to myself how inexpensive it seemed. Then I walked out of the gas station empty-handed and got back in my car. No, wait. I bought cigarettes and a lemonade, the cost of which exceeded the price of the windshield-washing fluid. This is all just to give you an idea.

I used to drive in sandals. Adidas. The kind favored by indoor soccer players, those kings of the ninth grade. The kind with pebbled rubber soles. The kind that take some getting used to. I would walk circles around my apartment, mincing about gingerly as the rubber nubs stuck like needles into my flesh. I wanted to sand away my calluses.

That was the year that I was working toward physical perfection: flawless skin, a minimum BMI, a haircut that suited me, a hair color that suited me, a wardrobe that suggested something. I had been wearing the same clothes since the Great Back to School Shopping Spree of '06. My clothes were weary of me. They longed to retire to my childhood closet, along with my Hartford Whalers jacket and the cowboy boots I swore I would wear.

I bought the clothes in one dizzying spree. At the first two stores I was sure the saleswomen were interested in me sexually. By the third store I caught on. I considered myself street smart. I knew not to tip female bartenders too much. I had been to my fair share of strip clubs. I didn't consider myself a rube. Then again, I was shopping with my grandmother's credit card after I lied and told her I had an important job interview.

I did sit-ups on the floor of my apartment, my toes jammed under the front of the couch. I did push-ups over a white towel in front of the television. I ate vegetables until my piss stank. I set the fire alarm off three nights in a row, cooking chicken breasts on the stove top. When I stopped for fast food I got only half of what I wanted. I bought a monthly plan at the tanning salon. After I gave myself a severe pubic buzz, I scheduled a consultation with a body-hair removal specialist. After that, I bought a beard trimmer and just did what I could reach. This inspired a new stretching routine. Lasers are expensive.

Diet and exercise and eight hundred dollars at the outlet mall. Razor-burned shoulders. An eye-catching home dye job. Soles as smooth as sea glass. Expensive tortoiseshell sunglasses, loose on my face, sliding down the red bridge of my nose. In the parking lot of the public beach I took stock of my recent achievements and self-improvements, counting my pores in the rearview mirror. I was taking the new me on a test drive. The bathing suit I had sent away for was smaller than I would have liked. Small enough that I was concerned about penis cleavage. Small enough that I felt the need to work myself out a little bit there in the car, as the sun beat through the windshield and into the fake-leather interior, hiding behind the same windows I shield myself with today. Stepping out of the car I arranged my towel like a snake around my neck and pushed my shades back up over my eyes. I tried to walk with my head tilted up in order to keep the glasses from backsliding. The parking lot was above the beach and there were steep wooden stairs that were crowded with people walking up and down with coolers and children and folding chairs. I kept my head up, even amid the chorus of Watch Where You're Going's.

The beach itself was breathtaking. I wondered why I didn't come more often. This was the sort of indulgence that would clear my mind and allow me to wash my car on the way home from work. I had trouble walking in my sandals in the sand, so I plucked them off and carried them in my free hand. My other hand held my reading material, carefully selected to signal both literary taste and a lack of pretentiousness. It was the book that everybody had been reading the previous Christmas. If anyone asked, I was going to say that I was reading it for the second time.

I found a good spot, close enough to a trio of girls that I could admire the droplets of sweat roll down their glossy stomachs, but not so close as to draw attention to myself. My towel was lumpy. Everyone else seemed to have them pulled as tight as hospital bed sheets. I lay down, the hillocks of sand punching my back like a massaging chair. The sun felt close. It took up my entire field of vision. I blocked it with my open book. My arms began to tire. In the new shade I glanced down my body toward the ocean. My feet were shooting straight up. They were capped with ugly yellow toenails. The things we ignore, I thought, when we try to improve ourselves.

A man on a motorcycle, bright yellow with an angry whine, snakes between the rows of stagnant automobiles. When I was a sophomore in college my roommate won a motorcycle just like that one during a game of bingo at the local casino. He met a girl and moved out before the semester was half over.

I have nothing against clipping my toenails. I just don't like the sound it makes when you break through a thick one. It sounds like a butcher shop and it reminds me of the helplessness of death, how you can't feel anything. One time I was alone in a sauna and I was clipping my toenails, keeping the shards in a small pile next to me. While attacking a particularly stubborn nail a shard flew like shrapnel into the basket of hot coals. For a minute I was proud of myself. It was like spitting into a spittoon. Plus there was an element of revenge. Burn in hell, I may have said out loud. I sat for a moment thinking of something else when I noticed the smell. It was an indescribably human smell. A small part of me was being cremated. The toenail clipping was in the midst of the sublime pleasure that is the last laugh. I retied my towel and gathered my pile in preparation to make a hasty departure when the door opened and three other men I knew entered the sauna. We exchanged our peculiar locker-room greetings (Ed McMahon's "Hey-oh!" all around) and I settled back down. They all remarked on how soothing the heat felt on their tired muscles, and then they all took deep, relaxing, satisfying breaths.

My God, what is that smell? One of them exclaimed. Everyone turned to look at me. My life flashed before my eyes, faster than it does now, focusing more on successfully completed sex acts, on Michelin-rated restaurants I have found myself in: Energetic fellatio from Bree in Las Vegas, the crème brulée from Commander's Palace. The crimson began to build in the back of my neck.

I know, I said. Can you believe it? I've been trying to figure it out for a while now. I could actually hear the toenail sizzling. I snuck a glance over. There it was, on top of a red-tipped coal. It looked partially melted, black on the corners, like an onion slice left too long on a summertime grill.

It's absolutely disgusting, said someone. We all agreed. It was unacceptable. And then, because we were men, we stayed in the sauna, the temperature rising, the sweat trickling down from our heads, until the smell faded away.

Those girls' stomachs were not so much pink as they were the orange of a clementine placed in a lunch bag and left at the office over the weekend. There was a ripeness to their appearance.

Holy shit, said one of them, apropos of nothing. The words slid out, not as a reaction to any shock or surprise, but as a lazy commentary on the state of the world at that moment, as it appeared to her. One of them smoked a cigarette with a sneer, looking as if she had ignored the old wives' tale about unpleasant facial expressions sticking around longer than you might like them to. And one of them was quiet, black hair endlessly shiny. She looked familiar, sitting in her beach chair, back reclined at the same angle as a first-class airplane seat at 35,000. There was a flutter somewhere in my chest. The last time I felt that way it had, of course, ended disastrously. But I had taken quite a risk, playing that song in front of the entire school, naming her explicitly in the refrain. Later that day, after school, I had gone to her job at a high-end store that was popular with the girls in our grade. Almost everything was either bright pink or lime green. I thought immediately of diarrhea medicines. I asked the woman at the counter if she was around and the woman said, hold on a minute, and went into the back. I felt the same way you feel at the doctor's office. Not so much in the lobby as just after, when the nurse has taken your temperature and your blood pressure, weighed you and marked your height. And then she says, take off everything but your undies. The doctor will be along in just a minute.

That was the feeling I had had, standing in the fluorescent storeroom, waiting for the girl to emerge from the employees-only area. The same as when you sit on the leather bed with the paper sheet that crinkles noisily when you shift your weight, those multicolored pamphlets about pregnancy and warts and asthma and diabetes screaming at you from the wall, everything that can go wrong explained in graphics and bullet points. You think, well, if my own body can betray me like that, what could someone else do? Imagine the damage another person could inflict on this, the most fragile and essential of organs. Imagine how free they would feel to inflict that pain, when all they had to do was walk away. It would be just like clipping a nail. You would become, at best, something vestigial. Something inessential that was bothersome and then removed. The door to the employees-only area swung open.

I felt my blood tingle as it rose to the surface again. It was too hot on the beach for shame. The ocean looked inviting, a good place to hide. After some deliberation I removed my shades and placed them next to my book, on top of my towel. I'd read the first two sentences of the first page of the novel. Just those twenty-odd words had left me cold, lonely. It was simply well-written escape. I had been looking for a friend.

On the walk to the waterline I felt sturdy. The sand hardened as I got closer. While I felt the six eyes of the girls on my back, I tried to remember what my grandmother had always said whenever I accompanied her to her club and she introduced me to the grandchildren of her friends and made me join them for tennis or golf or, the worst, swimming lessons. I would beg her to let me go home. I said it could be my birthday present, my Christmas present, my birthday *and* Christmas present. Relax, she always said. No one is going to pay any attention to you. And she was almost always right. I would join them for doubles and watch long rallies between the three of them, occasionally twisting my body to avoid an overhead swatted in my direction. I would join them for golf and hit my drives directly into the woods and by the time I emerged with a ball they would be on to the next hole. During swimming lessons I tried to stay underwater as much as possible.

One time I came to visit and didn't bring along a bathing suit, hoping that this would get me out of it. Nonsense, said my grandmother, they have millions of them just lying around. She asked our waiter, who asked someone else, who brought a plastic bag to our lunch table. Inside was a pair of swimming briefs, as ugly and ill-fitting as the extra sport coat they have hanging in the dining room closet for sloppy stepsons. When I walked out of the locker room wearing that Speedo the other children stopped and stared. I was fifteen. My penis skipped a beat.

I plunged into the ocean, tripping over a wave. The cold surf knocked the country club Speedo back into my subconscious, where I was sure it would stay until later that night when I laid in bed and recounted the day, after the wine and Lean Cuisine(s) and dating site(s). The pleasure of delaying the inevitable is one of the pleasures I hold most dear. It gets me through most of the day.

I love to keep my eyes open underwater—the sting of the salt, the idea that I am seeing something I should not be, or just the fact that it is a parallel world, both familiar and not, with different creatures and shapes and a different colored light, a light accepted and dismantled. I can't stay down there too long. I tried snorkeling once and found it terrifying.

Maybe that's how Sadie the shop girl felt in the storeroom, always looking over my shoulder at the door, her ear cocked for the bell that alerted them to entering customers. She seemed as frightened as a trapped animal, ready to chew off the tail that kept her there. Instead she nibbled her thumbnail.

When I came up for air, for a moment there was nothing to see but the wide clear burn of the sky. The girls were twenty yards from where I floated, elbows crooked around their knees. It felt good to have them in front of me. Now they were on display, full of vulnerabilities. For starters, that dark bump between their legs. And the waxy shine of their skin where the UV rays haven't flashed over like a Xerox machine. And now they had to wonder what to do with their hands. I noticed the smoker light a fresh cigarette. They are not immune. Their imperfections are just smaller, easier to hide; a single errant hair, rather than a forest spreading across the shoulders. It's not that the stakes aren't higher, only that there is less plucking to do.

An ambulance screeches by in the break down lane. I edge as far to the right as I can manage. Most of my fellow motorists do not even glance over. I assume we all know that one day we will get that ride. No sense in being jealous today.

I recall Sadie as nearly perfect, economical in her movements and speech, long-limbed and clear-eyed, with thin eyebrows that stayed completely flat. I often wished that I could see the world through those eyes, the way obstacles and annoyances were ushered offstage moments before she entered. I stayed up late and wrote song lyrics about her in thick journals that I insist on keeping in a drawer, despite the pain they cause me when I overdose on wine and underdose on Lean Cuisine and break out the journals and flip page after page. My band, Sweatband, petitioned the student council and we were given half of an assembly to play for the school.

I realized later, after hiding in the janitor's office for most of the day, arranging piles of sawdust and spinning the table vise open and closed, that the problem with the song we played, what caused the open jaws and projectile laughter was the perspective from which the song was written. I had thought that it would be clever to write the song about Sadie and I from a possible future, when we are in the midst of a rough patch, both of us needing to prove ourselves worthy of each other.

*You call me up, it's late at night/ Over and over again/ You've got the will and I've got time to fight/ Over and over again*

I had thought that by forcing her to imagine a world where we were already together we would instantly come that much closer to the realm of possibility. Instead it was received as a basement dweller's fantasy. The hallway reviews were vicious.

My mother had taught me how to tie a bandana around my head, which I kept in my locker until assembly, and then wore onstage. Luke, the lead guitarist, wore a vest with no shirt on underneath, though not a leather vest. When confronted later about the vest he admitted that it had been part of a Boy Scouts uniform that he had stripped of badges the night before. Kevin, on the drums, wore beads around his neck, and several sweat bands crept up both his wrists.

I plunged back into the water and raked my fingers across the ocean floor. I blew bubbles out of my nostrils and watched them rise to the surface. Eventually, inevitably, I followed. I swore I could smell the sharp thin smoke of the girl's cigarette. I wanted to separate the black-haired sensible one from these sad imposters. I was always astonished at the way girls assembled themselves into precise, irregular triangles. They prowled the hallways as sharp as an arrow's head, but within the confines of the crew there is a clear alpha, beta, and hopeless hand-me-down who's older sister managed to shove in with a shoe horn. As a result, she agrees to steal the booze, covet no one, and do the heavy lifting required to keep up the creaseless life of a Sadie, or a black beauty, or a, I don't know, high school Caroline Kennedy.

Sadie eyed me across the floor as the Pepto-pink skirts hung silently on the racks. Cashmere sweaters bulged in piles on tables, full rainbows of cable-knit. She wore a polka-dotted headband. Her forehead was unlined.

Her sidekick was named Penelope. The hand-me-down was named Tova. Lacrosse players called them Win, Place, and Show. Penelope did ride horses, actually. I once ran into Tova in Beacon Hill. I was sleeping on couches, she was a senior at Tufts. She asked me how my music was going. I got the distinct impression that we could have slept together—third place, at long last—if only I had a bed to take her to.

I can see the ambulance's lights beating in the near distance, just a faint blue reaching out across the low sky. Make room. Make room. Danger. Danger. If only anyone ever told us how much, or how long it would linger.

I felt good enough to walk back to my towel, past the girls, after careful scrutiny of the genitals underwater to combat the shrinking effect of the chilly surf. Get half-hard despite the cold and then walk quickly through the breaks and take long strides against the undertow that pulls pebbles up and over your feet. That was the plan. I made my way through to the shallower side of the break. The girls seemed to be eyeing me, or just enjoying the view beyond me, a perfect, monochromatic horizon—who am I to distract from that? My grandmother was right, no one is looking at me. I thought, did I just jerk off underwater? I half-turned to admire the view myself when I saw the wave, the first of a powerful set. I pulled my legs forward as fast as I could, cursing my push-up routine, wondering why I hadn't asked for a Bowflex for Christmas, the undertow making my ankles disappear under an escaping tide. The first wave merely knocked me over. The second filled my bathing trunks with sand. The third removed them from my person completely, and swept them out to sea. When I emerged from the froth the girls were there, staring, expressionless as mannequins. They looked like Sadie, staring at her lime-green toenail polish as I asked her out. My Dad just got a new car, I said. The Peugeot is all mine now. Wherever you want to go. Wherever.

The sun is beating through the windows, melting the tint. The exit sign is suddenly nowhere to be seen. There might be other places I could go, but I can't turn around.

"I just want him to come already and get out of the room so I can lie there like an idiot holding my knees up in the air like I'm supposed to. You'd think it's a guy's dream, right? Just blow your load and get out. But no: he wants to act like he's in some kind of weird Christian porno, going really slowly, stroking my hair, telling me that he loves me. Jesus!" (Dee, page 21)

# Sunsets Over America

## Kevin Oberlin

If your sunset were painted less red
and unloaded from its U-Haul by men,
thick-gloved and hoping for quick pensions,
and nestled between the walls of your garage,
we'd sit on the lawn in spite of mosquitoes
on the blanket you knitted for our anniversary
and press the remote again and again
to make the colorless slats of the door
descend and rattle up again, each bend
an eruption, and then the full-on burn
of sunrise. I'd ask if you remembered
the way the sunsets in Cambridge seemed
cool by comparison, how they seared
the skies into darker blues, and the wind
carried them, puffs of cigarette smoke
over the roofs of the houses. Not so exotic,
really, roofs and houses and smoke and wind,
all things we have in Ohio. And yet
the sunsets here are always orange or ochre,
confusing themselves with dying leaves,
the horizon a muddle of wax, and we
cannot compete with our clearer memories.
We push the button to test the light
and wonder if when the door goes down
the sun goes out, or if it smolders.
Our neighbors peek out of their windows
to hush their dogs barking in wonder.

# Mum

## Leslie Maslow

ROGER IGNORED HIS MOTHER AND CURLED HIMSELF INTO A HOLE that Jacks, the family's Springer Spaniel, had dug under a pine tree. All week, she'd promised to take him to Dorney Park, but last night his mother suddenly announced that she was going to visit her great aunt at a nursing home near Philadelphia. Pulling her car onto Argyle Road, she called, "Be back tomorrow!"

How stupid to be left behind with Ellie, their housekeeper. The rattling engine faded into the distance. Roger wished he could stay there and let Jacks cover him with dirt, but he was too big. His teddy bear fit perfectly in the hole.

Paddington's arms stuck up toward him. Roger dropped handfuls of soil onto the smiling bear. He would show his parents that he did not need to carry around stuffed animals. His father complained that a boy of five and a half was too old for it. Roger liked this new sensation of burning in his throat and chest that came from holding back tears. He ran his hands over the earth to hide Paddington's grave.

Back inside, Roger crept through forbidden rooms seeking answers to why things were so different lately. Father was away at more and more conferences, like the one he was attending all this week. Roger poked his finger at the white puff of tissue paper stuffed in a hole over Mother's door handle. She used to bolt herself in until father had the lock removed. Even now, Mother kept the door shut and came out only when Father came home from his office at the end of the day. With a high, cheerful voice, she spoke of the small things that had happened, like the milkman forgetting eggs or a neighbor's new car. She presented her cheek to accept Father's kiss. Roger noticed that his father sniffed her face, like Jacks did to Roger whenever he got home from school.

At noon, Roger sat at the kitchen island eating mushroom soup while Ellie whistled and folded laundry. Thunder rolled in from across the tops of the trees. The washing machine, out of balance, started thudding against the dryer. The sky was dark, almost green. Jacks whimpered and paced in circles. The air felt still. Ellie's whistling ceased.

"Ellie?" he said.

His heart pounded. The swinging door to the dining room swelled outward as if a ghost was trying to enter. He ran into the laundry room.

"Ellie?" he called again.

The ironing board stood abandoned.

A sudden upward gush of air passed through the open windows. Rain hissed on the hot pavement of the driveway. It smelled like someone had struck a match. On the kitchen table, papers came to life and slid off as if they were escaping. A door slammed. It sounded to him as if someone was rolling a bowling ball around upstairs.

Ellie ran inside, the mail clutched to her chest, her uniform plastered to her back. She began waving a damp catalog in the air. The last time he'd seen Ellie spread mail on the table had been during the week of his parents' big anniversary trip. They'd planned to be gone for three weeks. But on a Friday at the end of the first week while Ellie and Bill, the lawn man, drank coffee at the kitchen table, his parents walked in the front door. Ellie and Bill stood up immediately. Bill left the house without a word. Normally his father would have lectured them, but this time both he and Roger's mother walked through the kitchen and upstairs with pasted-on smiles, like they were *pretending*.

Other strange things happened this year. Nobody swam in the pool yet except for Roger, even though the Fourth of July was coming soon. In the past, his mother would bring her little radio and stretch out on the lawn chair with a plastic pince-nez over her eyes, angling a fan of silver foil toward her face. His father would join them in plaid swim trunks, cannonballing off the diving board. This summer, the only company Roger had while he paddled around was Bill, skimming the surface of the pool with a long-handled net, or Ellie, soaking her feet on the pool ladder.

This year, too, Roger kept a secret. He had always loved to sit on the carpet next to the sideboard in the dining room and admire silver pieces on the shelves. One day he noticed that a sugar bowl with four feet was missing. The tongs for the sugar cubes lay forgotten in the back of the cabinet. The next time he looked, the tongs and six silver napkin rings had vanished. He inspected the sideboard and could not find the little silver cup that bore his initials, RFS, and the date of his birth. He tiptoed up to his mother while she was watching television and asked about it.

It was then that he and his mother began their special pact.

"Mum's the word," she whispered, her breath on his face.

"Mum?" he asked.

"It means if anyone asks, you don't know anything," she said.

For the first time, she smiled at him the way she smiled at grown ups.

"Oh, yeah," he said.

She tugged the zipper on his jacket.

"You know what you are?" she asked.

From her adoring eyes, he could see it was something good, something wonderful.

"One cool cookie," she said.

She released his coat and flopped back against the couch. This time, she let him sit up on the cushion next to her. She fondled his hand with both of hers and explained that the missing silver was a test she had devised for Ellie to make sure she wasn't pawning family heirlooms. Roger didn't understand, but he didn't care. He and his mother were friends now.

He searched for more missing items so they could keep being friends. Once he discovered an empty glass behind a potted plant, but that was it. Nothing had disappeared from the sideboard in a long time, and the closeness he had enjoyed with his mother faded.

He slid down from the chair to tell Ellie he'd finished his soup, but, seeing her lips moving, he stopped. Father had explained to Roger that Ellie's lips moved that way when she aired her "inside thoughts." The way his father said it, there was something silly about it, that it was like when Jacks tried to bite car tires.

At this memory, he felt an ache in his stomach. Ellie was not his mother or father. She was a worker, paid to be in the house with him. She was a word his father had taught him: an *employee*.

Roger went to the screen door and gazed at the weeds growing between the bricks in the patio. The thunder rolled away beyond the kennel, over the field and out past the old logging road that led through the woods. The storm was still happening, he thought, but it wasn't happening here anymore. He might as well go dig up Paddington. No one would be back that day to care if he held on to baby-toys or not.

A new idea hit him. He pressed his palms into the sagging mesh of the screen door. *What if his parents had left him and they were never coming back?*

Maybe this was why, all spring, the house was slowly being emptied of the silver. Maybe it was why cobwebs gathered in the corners of rooms and why his mother took long drives when she could no longer lock herself in her bedroom. Or why Father had started attending more and more conferences—maybe he wasn't even going to conferences, but to find a new house that they would live in. Without him. It could explain the tree limbs fallen on the yard, and the dandelions, and Bill only coming three days a week instead of five. It could explain Ellie talking on the phone more often, being more kindly toward him than scolding.

Maybe his parents had planned this all along.

Ellie must know they had gone. But if he asked, she would say it wasn't true. And then he would be unsure again. No. Better to feel the tearing inside that he felt now, than to have hope. Dumb, baby hope belonged in that grave with Paddington. He would find out for himself. He would go in the basement and see if the suitcases were gone.

"Ellie? Will you come to the playroom with me?" he asked.

"In a minute, hon," she said.

He sat at the top of the stairs to the basement waiting for her. A damp waft of cool air hit him from below. He edged his way down the steps on his bottom until he was able to peer into the room.

"Ellie!" he called.

"In a minute!" she answered.

All he needed to do was look inside the boiler room to see if his mother's big trunk was there. But he had never gone down to the playroom alone. He was afraid of closets and utility rooms—shadows hid in them, like spiders and boogey men.

"Ellie!" he yelled.

He heard her muffled, angry words, then silence. He waited, the minutes growing longer. He'd gone too far. Now she wouldn't come. He forced himself to run down the remaining stairs and across the playroom to the door of the boiler room.

He opened the door and pushed until it thudded against a coiled garden hose. The boiler room, usually empty of the patio furniture in summertime, was a floor-to-ceiling puzzle of white chair frames. It was impossible for him to climb through the chaos where Father kept the suitcases. Raindrops rattled against the panes of a second door that led up a back staircase to the yard.

In the center of the room, something caught his eye. Two large patio tables were stacked, one upside down on top of the other. They were just over the drain hole. From underneath one of the tables peered his mother's face.

She wore a detached, pleasant expression, like the golden Buddha that sat on an end table in the living room. Roger saw something strange in his mother's features. Daylight gleaned off the vacant surface of her eyes. The lids closed. When they opened again, her eyes were looking right at him.

The pleasure slid off her face. Roger's legs were rubbery. His feet stuck to the ground. As his vision adjusted, he saw, below the face, two glowing domes. Naked knees. She was squatting under the table, directly over the drain. There was the sound of water. Tinkling.

Quick, so he wouldn't see any more, he leaned all his weight back, pulling at the doorknob. It was not right to see his mother doing that. But no, that was his *actual* mother he'd been thinking of. This creature and his mother could not be the same. His mother wore bright lipstick and shimmering blouses. This one seemed pale and sick. Maybe it was something bad, something pretending to be her.

It felt like forever as the door arced toward the frame and finally closed. In order for the door to lock, he had to push the button in, but it wouldn't stay. The tip of his finger began to hurt from holding down the button. He didn't think he could run across the basement to the stairs without risking the creature bursting out of the door and overtaking him. He might end up being kept in the basement with it.

Despite his terror, he felt sorry for her, whoever it was. She looked strange, but more familiar than anyone. But if it had been her, why didn't she say hello? Why did she act like he was a stranger?

The door shuddered against his back as if she was trying to get at him. He heard a slamming noise coming from inside. He screamed. His throat felt like it was ripping. Jacks bolted down the stairs. Ellie ran an obstacle course of a train set and scattered storybooks. She tried to pull Roger's hand away from the handle. He clawed at her forearm with his free hand. Jacks barked.

Hindered by his blubbering deep breaths, he tried to explain that he'd seen someone in the boiler room. Someone bad, threatening, pretending to be his mother.

"I thought we were supposed to be a big boy this weekend," Ellie said.

She breathed heavily and patted her forehead with a handkerchief. He thought she was annoyed because she had to come down the stairs.

"I saw it," Roger protested, feeling his anger rising.

"Honey, it's nothing to get worked up about."

"You don't know," he said.

Pushing the door open, she said, "I don't, do I?"

A nest of blankets lay next to the hot water heater. The edge of the cement pad was wet as if the door to the outside had recently been opened.

"Now, you see? Mommy's just playing her hiding game. We can leave her alone and not go looking for her, all right Roger? Tomorrow it'll all be back to normal," Ellie said.

Jacks wound his way through the jumble of lawn furniture and sniffed at the drain hole. He lifted his leg and urinated on the spot.

"Jacks!" Ellie scolded.

The dog looked at them, wagging his little motor of a tail.

Ellie stooped over and picked up an amber container next to the garden hose. It looked like the one he had seen in his father's bathroom. Father had taken big purple pills for his bad back. One remained in the vial.

"But, but it might not have been her," he said.

He pushed at his forehead with all ten fingers.

"Honey, don't get yourself worked up," she said.

"What if it was a robber?" he asked.

"It wasn't a robber."

But her voice sounded worried as she studied the container and put it in her pocket. She crossed the basement and began to mount the stairs ahead of him. Terrified he'd be left behind, he dashed past her, tripping and bruising his knees on the treads. The creature in the boiler room had imitated his mother. Who was to say that Ellie wasn't in on it herself? She might lock him down there too, for no reason.

Everywhere Ellie went, he followed, clinging. He wished he could have Paddington in his arms. The more she tried to chat the day away with a lighthearted tone, the more distressed he felt.

She spread a puzzle of a castle across the dining room table.

"Ellie?" Roger began.

"Look for the corners first," she said.

"Will you come outside with me?" he asked.

"Oh, honey. It's pouring rain. Help me find the corners," she replied.

"But I have to get Paddington."

After a few minutes of working on the puzzle together, Ellie pushed through the swinging door into the kitchen. He tried to follow her.

"I'm keeping the door open. I'm right here," she assured him.

He moved the pieces around. He couldn't concentrate. He kept turning around to see if someone was creeping up behind him.

In hushed tones, he thought he heard her say the name Bill. He had never heard her call Bill on the phone before. She lowered her voice but he heard her mumble "purple" and later, the brand of his mother's car, "Mercedes."

After a few minutes, Ellie hung up. She took the pill container from her pocket and hid it behind a cookbook.

"Who was that?"

"My daughter," Ellie said.

A lie!

As if to distract him, she began the ritual of making cookies. She took three eggs from the refrigerator and cracked them into a bowl. Usually she let him help. This time she didn't even think to ask for his assistance, but did it herself, mechanically, with a furrowed brow.

Roger wondered if Bill was in on it too. His father often checked to see if they drank from the tall bottles. This must have been because he didn't trust them. Sometimes they did pretend they were working when they were sitting at the kitchen table having coffee.

A shaft of sunlight cut across the island.

Opening the screen door, Ellie held his hand and walked across the grass to the clothesline. Jacks bounced ahead of them. The air was cool and clean. It felt strange pretending that everything was normal; he had a sense that the two of them were both going along with someone's plan. They could hold hands and walk together because they were not actually enemies; the feeling was more that they were playing for different teams.

The sun dropped behind the trees, turning the branches black against the sky. The white brick building behind the house was cast in a peach-colored light. The previous owners had used part of it as a kennel, and Roger sometimes liked to crawl up the ramp on all fours and play inside the cages.

Ellie snapped and folded a wet sheet that had been left out in the rain. Roger crept around the corner of the building, hunting for Jacks' tennis ball in the weeds. Shadows moved down his arms. A flock of starlings plummeted toward the roof and lifted, shifting their shape against the dusk.

Roger wished dogs were staying in the kennel. He thought of last winter, when an elderly neighbor on Argyle Road had died in his garage with the car running. The man had left behind two fat old Boxers. Father housed them in the kennel until new owners adopted them. The building felt lonely without them. He looked at the orange sunlight reflecting off the row of windows.

"Roger!" Ellie called.

Her voice evaporated into the air. He waded through the grass. He could hear nothing but his breath in his ears. In the sea of green, he stopped, remembering what he had just witnessed.

One of the windows was open.

A chilly, wet feeling crept down between his shoulder blades. Father was very strict about keeping the kennel locked. He turned back to it. The windows looked like they were on fire. Halfway down the row, a narrow black slit interrupted the blazing line.

Ellie's voice sounded close now, "Let's go inside and make dinner, honey."

He stepped onto the lawn and took her hand. Ellie led them toward the screen door. He did not turn back to look at the kennel. He did not need to. He knew that his mother was there.

Now he remembered. It *had* happened before, like Ellie said. One night, Mother had screamed at Father: she'd slammed the door and left the house crying, dropping blankets and clothes as she stumbled across the yard to the kennel. He'd watched his father stand at one of the open windows, begging her to come back in the house. Father wasn't here now. Only Ellie. He didn't know what to do. He didn't think he could face this strange, altered mother alone.

His teeth chattered. Ellie put her hand on his head.

"Some nice pigs-in-a-blanket will warm you up," she soothed.

That night, he asked Ellie to let him sleep in her warm yellow room with the slanted roof at the top of the house.

"Your father would be upset with me," she said.

"I won't say anything," he promised.

"That would be a lie, then, wouldn't it?" she said.

"No it wouldn't. It would just be like . . . It would just be like when you keep mum," he said.

Never before had he mentioned his mother's pact to anyone. He felt guilty, like he was giving away something special.

"Mum," she said. "Where did you learn that?"

"Patrick," he said, naming a boy from down the road.

Ellie made the clicking sound she used when cars drove too close behind her. This time, she meant it for Mother.

In the night, he woke up to snores sounding like fabric being torn. The room was bathed in silver light from the full moon. White showed under Ellie's half-closed eyelids. Her mouth puckered like a fish every time she inhaled. He reached out to touch her shoulder but brought it back. He knew from trying that he couldn't bring people out of sleep. They were somewhere far away. If he woke them, they would be angry and the distant place would remain in their eyes. It only made him feel lonelier.

Each of her snores jolted him from sleep, letting him down, hurting him, abandoning him. He remembered her phone call earlier in the day. She'd turned away from him and lowered her voice. A new idea came to him: maybe Ellie and Bill had tied his mother up. She was being kept against her will. He imagined how terribly hungry she must be after all this time. If they were truly up to no good, he had the chance to save his mother. He could be more grown up than he'd ever been before. A wild, impatient hope sprang up in him. It was not that his parents had abandoned him; it was Ellie and Bill who had taken advantage, stolen silver, and neglected the house.

If this were true, then his mother would be relieved when he went to her to set her free. She would be overcome with joy. She would take him in her arms and hug him, rocking him back and forth, thanking him, petting his head, her eyes shining with gratitude. To think that he'd waited this long, while she was out there, trapped!

He tiptoed downstairs to the laundry room. Jacks lay there, warm, curled into himself. Sensing Roger's presence, the dog rose, shook himself and began sneezing with excitement by the screen door.

"Do you know too?" he whispered.

He climbed a wooden stool in the pantry and took down a box of cereal with a jogging, smiling couple on the front. He dropped some of Ellie's chocolate chip cookies into the box, then slid open the door.

He edged his way along the kennel toward the ramp and doggie door at the far end of the building. Reaching the ramp, he stopped and held his breath. There, in front of him, so close he could reach out and touch it, was a large, glowing object.

It was his mother's car. Silver, covered in dew. It was concealed by the grass and faced the house, like she'd driven from the direction of the field, on the old logging road.

Pinning the cereal box under his arm, he crawled up the ramp, leaving a trail of spilled cookies that Jacks choked back as he followed behind. Inside, Roger felt his way along the full-sized cages lining the sides of the kennel. A pigeon fluttered, rearranging itself in the rafters. He moved toward a dim, red light. His heart beat with hope. For many long months, he'd felt mother falling away from him. Now, he was going to save her. She would be forever grateful.

A heat lamp cast an orange glow onto a sleeping human figure, curled on one side. Her knees were slightly bent, tucked under the hem of a sweatshirt that read "Penn State."

Mother did not wheeze and heave in slumber like Ellie; she did not move at all. There was a small circle of dried vomit on the floor in front of her mouth.

"Mommy!" he cried.

Her head jerked. She lifted it as if she was balancing a glass of water on the upright temple. An inch, then another, then another, until she was vertical enough to begin turning toward him. She stiffened her arms to prop herself up. He searched inside the box for a cookie to give her.

"Are you hungry?" he asked.

His voice sounded hoarse. There was so much he wanted to say, but seeing her, he was struck dumb.

Her hair trembled around her face. She traced the perimeter of her mouth with her tongue. In the light, it looked black.

He dug his hand into the cereal box, finding only loose flakes at the bottom. She stared at him like she was trying to figure out who he was. His fantasy of being the great rescuer was slipping away. He told himself that all he had to do was the right thing, the perfect thing.

"I brought you cookies, but they fell out," he said.

He reached his fist toward her. Cereal dropped through his fingers onto the floor. He inhaled in deep, shivering breaths. Warm tears moved down his cheeks. He was failing.

Her voice croaked out of chapped lips, saying something he could not understand. She banged her fists against the ground like a child deprived of a toy. He moved toward her. Before he even settled onto his knees, he felt her palm pushing through the front of his pajamas. He fell backward against something warm and soft—Jacks, who yelped. Roger gripped the chain link of the cage. He saw Mother pressing her hand into her eye.

"Can't you just give me one god-damned night?" she begged.

She wiped her mouth and hinged back onto the straw bed, facing away from him.

He felt like someone had rung a giant bell over his head. He could hear nothing but the ringing and could barely command his legs to move in stiff, electric jolts away from her. He barreled through the tall grass. Halfway up the back staircase to Ellie's room, he sat down. Ellie's snores ripped through the air, taunting him from above. Everything felt like it was collapsing in on him.

He closed his eyes and let his body go heavy while his fists gripped the spindles of the banister.

He seemed to be falling down a well. At the bottom, moving toward him, he saw a glowing black sun. It soothed him. He wouldn't bother his mother anymore. She would miss him, but she could never have him back. After a time, his hands relaxed. He wedged his back against the stair and fell asleep.

In the morning, a wet nose sniffed Roger's ankle. Jacks wagged his entire body with the pleasure of the new day. Ellie lifted him into her arms, whispering about pancakes. She tried to draw Roger out. He pretended for her, a little, so that she might leave him alone.

After breakfast, he waited on the driveway with Ellie. The rattling engine returned. When Mother stepped out of the car, Ellie muttered something to her about lateness. His mother wore the same skirt and silk blouse that she'd worn the day before. Strands of her hair draped across her cheek and stuck to the freshly applied color on her lips. Her hand shook as she pushed the car door closed. Ellie searched her face as if she needed to decide something before she could hurry off to church. Mother made herself tall, so that Ellie pulled back. Ellie got into her Beetle and drove off.

Mother held out a shopping bag to him.

"Hey there, little partner. Got ya a present," she said.

He felt himself being pulled by some invisible energy toward her, but a stronger energy pulled him away. He was tempted to ignore the bag she offered him and walk off, but he knew that would have been an invitation for false apologies. What difference did it make?

He took it.

Mother brushed her hand against his cheek and tottered through the breezeway and into the house with a blanket in her arms. She hooked her shoe around the edge of the door and pulled it closed, accidentally slamming it. Father's swordfish, mounted above a long antique wooden bench next to the door, slid down and wedged itself between the bench and the wall.

He lifted the present from the bag. He recognized the blue coat, the yellow hat. Paddington. Given to him not because he'd buried his beloved friend, for she could not have known that. Not because she wanted to defy his father's wish that he outgrow his toy either. Not because Ellie steam cleaned the old one monthly, under Father's orders. In the sparkling, cloudless June morning he knew why his mother had done it; she didn't remember there had ever even been a Paddington.

He lowered the bear back into the bag and sat on the warm driveway, staring off toward the swing set. The bright green leaves of a birch tree waved back and forth at him in the breeze, tittering. He felt like he might float up in the air. His mother didn't really notice him. She cared only for herself. The relief of this made him want to laugh, to scream in joy.

He dropped the bag, remembering that he'd left the real Paddington out in the rain all night.

While his mother slept and Ellie fanned herself at church, he took a gardening trowel from the garage and re-buried Paddington good and deep, so that Jacks wouldn't unearth his secret. He took the phony bear into his room and placed it on his highest shelf. Father would say he was a big boy to give him up, not realizing that the clean one was only a decoy. He wouldn't touch it. He wouldn't look at it. And his mother would see.

# To Jorge in Sickness

James Schuyler

You are sick in a hotel in Norfolk;
the weather there is fine: full of medicine and fever,
you may drive to a beach and I suppose walk on it.
Here, it has rained for three days.
The day is cold and opaline. It is Sunday.
I will bathe, dress, and go see my friend John.
As I told you, we are writing something together.
I have so much to do. Most won't get done:
"first things first" "there are just so many hours to a day"
and I miss you
and am worried
"you must bundle up warm" "not over-do"
and I think how I might be there walking on a beach with you
in gauzy light and the medicated smell of the ocean
on the shadows of gulls
sliding silently on the sand as love
goes from us like a bird-shadow, or a desire for flight:

for my dual emotion
is to walk with you there in sunlight, which is love,
and to fly not from here but myself, which is childish.
Childish I am, you know, but if it is I you at all love,
let me wish what in my emotion is not child-like but childish
away and play at patiently
waiting your getting better and coming back.
Here the weather is ugly and smokey.
There the weather is clear and fine.

We talked on Sunday on an extravagant invention,
the telephone: I miss you.
Beware of bone-tiredness
that brings sickness.

James Schuyler

# It's Nice Inside When It Snows

Self-conscious and up-to-date,
kissing by lamplight,
whatever it was, it was not for that,
whatever it is, it is not for this.

These are ugly chairs.
These are comfortable chairs.
This has an unnecessary dimension.

Its name is necessity.
Its name is beauty.

Firelight eats shadows in the wall.
A mirror in the hall
shows firelight shining from wall to wall.
Firelight devours the mirror in the hall.

They hold each other.
They laugh, kiss and tell
what they have themselves
to tell, or not to tell.

# Birdland (or Caligula-Caligulee, or Come Into the Garden Maud, the Grass Needs Mowing)

NOIA: Now I am going to dance. I am going to dance a good long time. I am going to dance very slowly and clumsily. I am going to dance just as much as I please. It is going to be very boring for all you out there. I don't care.

I am going to dance anyway.

CAPTIVE AUDIENCE: A-a-a-a-a-h!

VOICE FROM THE REAR: Take it off! Take it off!

(enter the Goodman brothers with each other's heads on duraluminum platters. The swing duet from Messager's *Veronique* tunes in)

CAPTIVE AUDIENCE: Kill that woman!

NOIA: I am still dancing! (and so dies Noia, Princess of Bavaria, crushed beneath the windshield of her own Thunderbird).

As the curtain tenderly falls, the bird audience, released from its cage, twitters, *e pluribus unum...il mondo e fango...il faut tenter...nudus amor formae non amat artificem...de cette nuit, Phénice...to waft her love...*

and the lights come up

James Schuyler

# Small Talk

—I hear there's a drought.
—I can live without that.
—Did you see *Blow-Up*?
—I found it quite old hat.
—What do you think
  of the new morality?
—I think undergrads
  should concentrate on their grades.
—You may be right.
—I could be wrong.
—What a sweet
  thing to say.
—Compliments are never out of date
  if they're sincere.
—About the new morality
  I don't know much
  but I love
  the old sincerity:
  Are you for real?
—I guess I'm kind of
  out of date
  but right from the start
  I like to speak
  from the heart.
  At any rate
  let me feel your nose:
—A cold nose

means a warm heart.
My, your nose is hot.
—What's worse
I've got cold feet.
Cold feet?
In those shoes?
What kind of foot powder
do you use?
—Dr. Scholls.
—Well, that's the best.
have you tried
lamb's wool liners?
I'm allergic
to wool.
—So that's your Achilles heel.

# Nevada City Diary

## Louis B. Jones

Cold Christmas of 2008. News is of Israelis bombing Palestinians, and of economic depression worldwide. Deep snow here in the mountains. At the ATM machine of Wells Fargo bank, while I stood waiting for it to grind and clank and deliver my money, I watched an ant (one of the small, coppery-black Argentine variety) come out of the INSERT YOUR CARD slot and immediately reenter the bank by the TAKE YOUR STATEMENT slot.

****

Late fall: The field mouse and the bulldozer:
Barbara's cottage will require its own septic tank, and there's been a bulldozer/backhoe in the meadow this week, excavating for a new leach field. For some reason, the machine that was rented is as big as a tyrannosaurus rex, looming up higher than the garage. Yesterday morning with dew still on the grass, the operator got the diesel engine running and began ranging all around and, first of all, plucked out of its foundations Dashiell's old iron swing set, because it was in the way—and then suddenly I became aware that he'd leapt off his high throne, climbing down out of the cab, saying *Poor little guy!* and he was creeping up on the foundation of Barbara's new cottage, with handkerchief out. He'd scared a field mouse. In his handkerchief he brought it over to show me the frightened

refugee, its whole body as small as a strawberry, elegant gray fur, eyes like beads of caviar, little pink hands trembling. He took it over and set it down in the tall grass far from the job site, and scaled his machine again . . .

✳✳✳✳

Expensive Arborist comes to call: that pear tree is doomed.

The oaks are fine—this is just a particularly big year for the little green caterpillar, and those two-hundred-foot trees are in the prime of their lives.

No sign of leaf curl on the young peach. Have not sprayed this year.

✳✳✳✳

Pacific weather system keeps rain heavy. National Public Radio from the valley is slashed by static. Strange satisfactions of this pleasant so-called Recession. Idly Google-Earthing places I used to live, and even "street-viewing" them. They haven't changed. Someone else is there now, and it's fine for them to have it. Tonight in the kitchen, suddenly the compost bucket looked a lot like the soup stock pot, the one on the left, the other on the right. (One on the stove, one on the sink drain board.) The difference between the Saved and the Condemned is a personal judgment call. And one realizes this is not "hitting bottom," rather it's an inspired old innovation. Surely for thousands of years, grandmothers have had the same reflection.

✳✳✳✳

Used heavy-gauge "gopher wire" mesh to create a long enclosure to lower over the rows of broccoli. Weighted it down with several huge, heavy truck-tire chains. Still the rabbit can get to it, and nibble the plants to the ground. It's very uneconomical, this war I'm waging. I think I'll never recover the broccoli of yesteryear, the cauliflower of our first seasons here.

\*\*\*\*

Six o'clock in the afternoon. The last week of September in the great year of 2008. Glass of wine with Barbara in the meadow on wooden chairs after the carpenters' quitting time. How long will she live in the little cottage we're building for her? I look up and see a sight I realize I've always loved: there's an hour of evening when the topmost heights of the tallest pine trees are still in direct bright sun against sharp blue sky. It may be twilight and cold down here on the lawn—down here, a chill is coming over us—but up in the high branches it's still midday, it's still full summer.

\*\*\*\*

When I was young, spiders were ugly. The older I get, the more I can see it's a privilege to be in the room with one.

\*\*\*\*

My happiness is on these five acres. When I'm out at some desirable diversion, I count the minutes till I can get back.

\*\*\*\*

If we count up the "blessings" accorded us in our span of life—(wildflowers, the sight of stars, art and music of course, sex and all the seven cardinal sins, children, food, various colors such as leaf-green and sky-blue, the sensation of cold, the sensation of comfort, the knowledge of history and indeed the *sensation* of history moving in our bones, all of mathematics, sun on my shoulder, etc., blah blah blah, all these you might call, if not blessings, at least great good luck)—but the supreme blessing among them is surely our "self," our tenure of a "self," something of a "point of view" we can take, something separate from the vast pre-existent "*Other*"! To own a "self" (as it were in fee simple) is to have control of a small sovereignty *which is a bite out of the Eternal Other, an incursion into the Eternal Other*. In the economic metaphor that rules nature, a self collects the quantity "time" in a somehow separate fund. A fund parallel to eternity's larger account.

I'll say it again in a different way. We seem to discern this thing the "Other" (i.e., the rest of the universe). It definitely seems to be larger than ourselves, and it seems to have existed before us and will, apparently, exist after us. Within it we have a temporary freehold. We own this "self" only for a brief *duration* (as measured by the quantities it construes as "time"). The radical thing about this *self* is that it seems to contain—or at least behold—the infinite Other. This self *sees* the stars, as well as, moreover, the black spaces between the stars.

(The institution of a self seems to borrow not only from the time dimension but the space dimension too. The body's "*personal space*"—that is, the space inside my skin, including my heart and lungs and liver—seems for a lifespan an inalienable possession. A piece of three-dimensional territory.)

I've used the word "blessing." Of course supernatural or divine agencies aren't necessarily involved in our gaining a self. One is always aware that this "self" is a construction of nerve impulses that evolved in my species for species preservation, particularly for the sustenance of *society*, "society" being another evolutionary innovation, a survival strategy, which will help the species propagate and compete. The word "blessings" implies supernatural agencies. I might have called them simply a list of "good things," to placate those who are more comfortable in announcing skepticism. It is reassuring to go back to the scientific fact that all phenomena (the "self" as much as "the stars") arise naturally from Nature, via evolution. ————However, some see *nature* itself as supernatural. (That must be an ecstatic frame of mind!)

This is then THE fundamental false dichotomy to be deconstructed: the apparent "self/Other" opposition.

\*\*\*\*

How a Real Carpenter Moves Around a Job Site.

The widow Barbara's cottage is being built at the edge of our meadow, as August turns to September. Billy, Bruce, and Mike are (respectively) the master and journeyman and apprentice who arrive each morning, in pick-up trucks, with also a dog named Jed. They're our heroes. Each day after they've got in their pickup trucks and gone, we filter out onto the job site to see what miracles they've wrought in a day.

In the day it's ninety degrees, on that rink of plywood with no shade. A professional on a building site doesn't move with impatience, as I myself would (trying for "efficiency"). A professional has a slow, considerative way of traveling on the open floor, among the standing 2x4 studs, as if moving in a dream, moving through future-time. It's not just caution alone. It's a trance. It *is* future-time, there. In fact, I'm sure at night carpenters do dream of the job: they inhabit it so completely during the day, all day, each day, the nine hundred square feet of plywood platform within a little framework of standing golden 2x4s.

Just as I, myself, crawl into intractable little cramped spaces of my novel while I lie in bed, I'm sure they know those four rooms as well as I know my characters and plot, and at night they're back again on that plywood floor, crouching to drill into a stud for a plumbing vent, wrestling the Saws-All as it sabres a window opening in CDX, cheating the tub into place inside its cage of 2x4s. All day in the sun, in an eternal noon, tall and slow in their brimmed hats, leather belts swagging the heavy burden of hammers and pouches, when they move through the future they treat it tenderly and dreamily.

****

Bok choy has failed decisively. Not one sprout appeared. Have hoed up that row and will attach it to adjacent corn plot.

Corn, now, corn is exciting. Not like bok choy. Every kernel germi-
nates, and fast, so in a matter of days I see the entire complement of
thirty-six miniscule pale phalluses, not a single dud. Corn is an
experiment this year, but it already looks like it will be a success. I'm
planting so many because—as I understand—you need a lot of
them to get cross-germination, and they must be planted in three or
four rows to take advantage of the wind.

****

W.N.C.L.D.F.F.

"Western Nevada County League for the Discouragement of Film
Festivals."

****

Outside urban economy, how much painting there is to do. Scraper,
bucket, brush. Country-music on the radio. Here with wooden
buildings, the old-fashioned media prevail, window glazing with
putty, not HardiPlank siding or vinyl-covered windows. Wood is, by
comparison, such soft stuff. It's flesh. By the time you're done painting it all, it's time to start again. To maintain it requires, of one
man, a lot of painting.

****

Oakley, in these last weeks of his life, sat in our wicker chairs with
us, and kept mentioning the two immense trees at the far end of the
meadow, how well they were leafing out this year. He continues to
like gin and tonic but without the gin. It's about all he has. Of
course the obvious circumstance is that he will never see another
springtime. He keeps reverting to the subject of the pretty leaves.

When he was born in 1922, astronomers thought the universe con-
sisted of this little Milky Way galaxy only. Oakley would have been
taught in grade school (as I was too!) that our universe is an isolated cluster of stars, an island universe surrounded by a black void.

Louis B. Jones

And the black void, simply, "goes on forever." That was roughly the picture my generation got, too.

Now, especially since Hubble, we know that the universe is actually expanding, flying apart ever faster, so we're losing data and galaxies at the outer edges, but still, we can see *four hundred billion* (400,000,000,000) galaxies out there. What a universe to have lived in, during the period 1922–2008. And moreover what a place to be departing from, to sit on a meadow in, and admire two big oaks.

✳✳✳✳

The garden in March is a ruin, but there are still parsley and onions for Hunter's omelette Sunday night shared by all.

✳✳✳✳

[March 15. The experiment of freezing last summer's great tomatoes has failed. Brought out two of them from the freezer—they made a billiard-ball clack, knocked-together—but found when they thawed they collapsed into little wrinkly orange bags in a bowlful of their own water.]

✳✳✳✳

Back again on this topic of clotheslines and drying laundry in the sun.

I continue to sense myself at the brunt of an American avant garde when I wield wooden clothespins (British usage "clothes-pegs") in the meadow. I sense myself the cleverest fellow in the world. My dryer is idle. No sound of propane jets. Early this morning I was pinning up laundry again, in a parka, January sun just coming over the tops of the far pines. Economists are coining new words, or reviving old ones, to describe the mix of inflation and recession that is coming over us all as the consequence of our rapacious and stupid relationship with Mother Earth. Oil prices (but also prices of all raw materials including land) are driving up even the cost of broccoli and steak and have brought the Limits of Affluent Growth to our attention. The word "stag-flation" is being brought back from the seventies. Funny word.

A good word for what's coming is "impoverishment." In an econo-mist's sense, that is. Lack of wealth. Scarcity of resources and capi-tal. But it's not altogether bad news, because another fitting expres-sion would be "simpler living," wherein lies elegance. Also, the resources we continue to retain are our entrepreneurial and human-capital talents. So wealth is there.

That "putting up laundry" places me in an avant garde must sound pathetic. It's a grandmotherly expression. And I know well, there are still neighborhoods (for some reason I picture them in eastern states) where even "recycling" a little glass or aluminum is, still, a humiliation or an effeminacy or contemptible. I've been with peo-ple like that, and I know they're not bad people, not at all. I also know that my own sanctimonious holier-than-thou attitude on these topics, is a privilege of one who can afford the "off-the-grid" life of divorce from the corporate (or, for a word-and-book man, academic) job scene. And one who is happy to live modestly and work at all kinds of different things. My boys Hunter and Dash don't have all the latest coolest stuff, unfortunately. I know most folks need two huge jobs and total tie-in to all conventional institutions, just to keep up with normal. And I know I'm not keeping up with normal.

But it strikes me as rather a happy prospect that, soon, there will be fewer and fewer people trying to keep up with "normal." There will be fewer of us looking down upon the economic choices of folks in (ter-rible expression!) "third-world countries." Because I announce and declare now from the foothills, like Isaiah in my remote avant garde, we may already be a third-world country. Complete with a third-world country's classic "dual economy" unsupportive of a middle class.

****

More of Oakley: In the weeks before he died, sitting beside Barbara on the porch in the afternoon drinking tonic water w/out gin, he told her, "I'll be waiting for you sweetheart in my little carboard box on the mantlepiece."

****

That certain events "grow larger as they shrink into the past." ——
————————————————————Found myself using that expression in a letter of condolence to a friend of mine whose close relative had committed suicide. And then last night, I discover myself Googling "GLOCK, 9MM, CHROME" in "Google Images," because I wanted to get the details of a memory right. Long ago a screen-writer friend of mine displayed for me, from a desk drawer, the chrome-plated Glock nine-millimeter pistol he intended to use on himself one day. His first novel, thirty years earlier, was briefly on the best-seller list, and once he wrote and produced a major motion picture, still rentable in most video stores. His life in a rented apart-ment in Mill Valley. Upstairs from the coffee shop where he liked to hang out in the afternoons and "hold court." The poster on his apartment door of James Joyce (looking dapper and austere and unforgiving, legs crossed in a white-linen suit) had been there for twenty-five years. He later used the gun on his own stomach sitting in that same desk chair, where the window beside him had a view of the roof of the former Varney's Hardware just being transformed into a Banana Republic.

****

February 20.
From the point of view of environmental soundness, the citizens in the best position for creativity are the city folk, not us country peo-ple. The great possibilities for innovation (as well as probity) are in the cities. Out here, the mess is still being created and the old Romanticism still prevails.

****

February 21.
People who will find themselves somewhat plagiarized in my new novel, if they look close:

poet Charles Entrekin;
poet and anthropolgist Gary Snyder;
agriculturalist Wes Jackson;
my old workshop-mate of twenty-five years ago Lynne Schatz.

Let us see if, in the published book, they can detect ideas I took and
churned in.

✳✳✳✳

The Catholic catechism's radical mysticism, in chapter on tenth
commandment to avoid envy: the impoverished are to rejoice
because: "*To see is to possess.*"

Also this, elsewhere:
"*Modesty protects the mystery of persons and their love.*"

✳✳✳✳

September project. Needing a studio to work in, I was planning to
choose a spot in the woods to put up a "pole barn" (two-by-fours,
4x8 plywood, a dozen bags of cement mix, rolls of tar paper, a space
heater—all available at B&C Lumber). All one needs is a little place
far from the hilarity of family life, with a window.

However, Brett ran across a small ad: "*Shasta Trailer, 1953, $100.*"
One hundred dollars is about one tenth of the cost of the lumber-
yard materials listed above.

So the fellow who was selling it, down near Auburn, was happy to
haul it here himself (having pumped up the flaccid tires). Over the
years he'd been using it only as a hunting blind, dragging it to
places on back roads. Its last DMV registration was 1969, a year
when a great many things went unminded. My writing studio, now,
is teardrop-shaped in profile, two-wheeled, turquoise on the bottom
half, silvery on the top half, quilted aluminum, with birch-paneled
interior and cabinets. It lives now under the drippy oaks off the

edge of a somewhat lost meadow on the property. You have to look, if you want to see it. If you look straight at it, it tends to vanish.

John Cavendish, who knows how to do everything, came out of the woods to help me get it up level on cinderblocks. He not only knows how to do everything, he is, also, infinitely generous. Cavendish is another thing that in 1969 went unminded. (He was born here in this western town, son of a mining engineer, and he had started at Yale. But then went to the Woodstock festival, joined VISTA, etc., never looked back.) Cavendish arrived in the morning overequipped wearing his work gloves, bearing huge rusty iron house jacks, car jacks, a block and tackle, his own supply of cinderblocks. He has leveled many a trailer. I'd picked out some sloping ground, and my trailer's back end might need a small *tower* of cinder blocks. We backed it down the slope into place using Cavendish's four-wheel-drive with trailer hitch.

It's dry inside. I tore out the rickety Formica breakfast table (something more like a fold-away ironing board) and installed a solid table at the window, all of old, true two-by boards. Mouse shit. Open cardboard tray of D-Con's fluorescent pellets in the corner. I remember when I lived in Mill Valley and had received a small "forty pieces of silver" from a movie deal, I built a more opulent little studio, high on a hill, with a view above sequoia treetops, through leaded-glass windows. Writer "A" visited and noted that other writer "B" would be building *his* studio in Berkeley with a full bath—and that yet another writer friend, "C" in Orange County, has a backyard studio that is soundproofed and feng shui adjusted, and adobe! "A" suggested "studio envy" would come to plague a circle of writers. If they could see me now! Mine has a license plate. And a license plate frame, too, on the back end, with a witty joke for tailgaters *Stay Clear—My Rear Is Near*" announcing itself to anyone or anything in the depths of the forest behind who might think of following too close.

\*\*\*\*

Hemp Is Stronger than Iron.

It was time to cut down a stand of cedars. In so doing, I exposed some forest ground where my son discovered the frayed end of a buried length of rope, sticking up from the earth. (This is near where a barn is rumored to have once stood, as there is a squarish old foundation of stacked granite in those woods.)

By pulling the rope's protruding end, he was able to *unzip* the soil in a long meandering path, from its burial-horizon about two inches under the modern surface, lifting dirt clods wherever he went. Sixty feet later, at the ultimate end of the rope, a now-rusty nail (not a square nail; not that old) had been driven through the braids, once long ago, to fasten it against a tree or a post now long gone.

The nail had corroded, it was nothing but a flexible twig of black rust, while the hemp fibers were still strong and hard and resilient. I dried the whole sixty-foot length on the garden fence for a day or two, and put it away in the garage with other ropes, for future use.

****

February 23.
Last month Dash lost his first tooth and was awarded a silver dollar by the Tooth Fairy. Then, this week, another tooth came loose— (these things are smaller than the kernels at a corncob's tapering end)—so another coin appeared under his pillow. The two shiny coins have since been prodigally lost, somewhere among hoards of plastic toys. But the two discarded *baby teeth, they* have been archived, by my wife, in a ziplock baggie with a torn-off paper identifying them and dating them.

This morning I was reading in bed while Dash (as a seven-year-old will) wandered around the bedroom silently exploring drawers and cabinets and dresser tops, the mysteries of cufflinks and theatre ticket stubs, suspenders and big old boots. I was aware of him picking through the drawer of the little writing desk behind the bedroom door. Then he wandered away, toward other parts, wafting around the room, finally drifting down the corridor. It was about five minutes later that he drifted back to that drawer and said, with hesitation, softly but pointedly, "Dad? Why are my teeth in here?"

During that five minutes only silence had come from his bedroom. During that five minutes he, in his sovereign loneliness, was taking responsibility for the whole mysterious world. On the one hand, he had seen with his own eyes the gift of the Tooth Fairy, solid evidence of what a deserving boy he is and how ample the world is. On the other hand, there were the very teeth. I wasn't paying attention during that five minutes while he was totally quiet. He bore that weight because it's something children know they have to do, even in their darkest innocence. I think of it now in regard to my father-in-law's cheery anecdote—that his cardiologist in a jocular mood told him as he went off toward the oncologist, "Beware of oncologists, Oakley, they just want to make you feel good."

****

March 3.
The oldest pear tree on the east side of the house has, or rather did have, three main branches. Last summer, one of the three branches produced no fruit at all, and but little foliage. This winter, all that side's wood and twigs were clearly dead: the spurs were putting out no incipient buds. So during the February cold snap, I sawed off that whole branch, at its base, releasing a gallon of muddy rainwater that had been steeping like coffee in its hollow core.

Now April is coming, it's blossom time, and one of the two remaining branches is behaving just similarly.

****

March 20.
The neighborhood lion—a solitary female described as long-bodied and not so tall as a deer—has been spotted this spring on the road, and Hunter (who has loved the pre-dawn hike alone to the highway

school bus stop every morning, lighting his way on moonless winter mornings by the glow of his cell phone) now tends to stay in bed later, do some extra history reading, and let his mom fire up the minivan and scrape the windshield frost to drive him out to the road.

****

Cut down hundred-foot cedar with swift fine effective new Husqvarna 350 saw. Saved out two eight-foot lengths of the trunk for splitting into fenceposts. Rolled them up to the meadow and, with two iron wedges, split them lengthwise into posts, 6'x6'x8". Enlarged the garden enclosure by establishing new posts on the south side, sinking them three feet underground, leaving five feet of vertical cedar standing aboveground, and stapled up ten-gauge wire against the depredations of deer. Hung old gate from new gatepost, using the same old door hinges. Began tilling the new-enclosed earth and, at this point, Dash appeared. His videotaped cartoon shows must have ended. He turned on the irrigation spigot's rusty gush, to make mud in the new-tilled earth, while I fenced him in. Eventually he was flopping and tumbling in it, sitting in it, and squashing it into little castles. By dinnertime he could claim, rightly, that he looked like an orc, and had to be hosed off on the threshold before tiptoeing through the house to the bathtub, and I told him at dinner that today had been a good day because, ninety years from now, when he's old and gray and nodding by the fire and can't recall much about his life's ambitions and achievements—and doesn't even recognize anyone in the room with him anymore—he might yet remember with crystal clarity, as if it were right before his eyes, the great day when he was seven and played in the mud in the sun.

****

March 21.
Started tomatoes indoors, Brandywine and cherry. And planted one row of bok choy outdoors as an experiment. Lettuce, cabbage, onions, chard will go in tomorrow outdoors. Broccoli and cauliflower still to come. Potatoes and corn when frost is no longer a danger.

\*\*\*\*

March 24.

Today I parked behind the bookstore/café on the main street to walk around to the front for my double-cappuccino to go. On the parking pavement out back, all three waitress-barista girls were on their hands and knees—circled in a huddle—all wearing their ripped-denim skirts and other pretty gear, bare-shouldered or silk-shirted. They were following the dopey adventures of a small, dusty, brown thing that tumbled slowly there, a honeybee who had fallen into the cannister of powdered chocolate. The entire wait-staff was outside. Work at the "Wisdom Café" had come to a halt while they discussed whether to let him be, or "dump a glass of water on him," or find a little brush somewhere and poke at him, as meanwhile he blindly revolved.

\*\*\*\*

Religions make preposterous claims, but they are oddly practical claims.

Plenty of human institutions—art, for example, or poetry—are impractical looking. A number of successful, smart people go from cradle to grave without setting foot in a museum to look at a painting. Some care little about food, some are not meant for sensuality, or reading a poem. They get along fine.

In the case of a tried-and-true religion, if it's the real thing and not merely a pretext for racism or sexism or war, its practical result is (let's face it) to transform you into a saint and mystic. That's the inevitable point: sainthood and mysticism.

Since, in every full life, it is finally necessary to *be* a saint-and-mystic—yes, for every one of us; it's the sieve we're all inescapably ground through (most of us with the dignity of our privacy)—then a "religious" attitude of some sort becomes an inevitable necessity, whether homemade or off-the-rack.

There is a lot of talk these days—especially post-9/11—about the obvious deludedness of religion; how ridiculous religion is; as if one day we could all be rational! And overcome it! And everything would make sense! Such writers as Sam Harris and the author of *The God Delusion* are perhaps—I don't know—too young, or too wilfully pretending an innocence. They would say they don't believe a day will come when they'll have to be saints and mystics. They pretend, publicly, that they have no idea what such a bizarre warning could possibly mean.

Well, the fact is, maybe they will succeed in leading a life entirely on that level. Maybe some people do. Like those who live without art, without reading a book, without sex in some cases, without cuisine, and are perfectly happy and self-sufficient. Maybe they're übermenschen, those Christopher Hitchens types.

Christopher Hitchens is a marvelous rhetorician, always a pleasure to read, and a lively entertainment personality. But one with an interest in "truth" or "verity," of some kind, ought not to go to an entertainment personality for it. Mr. Hitchens has some unexamined assumptions. A useful way of defining God is: "a necessary logical assumption." "A first logical assumption." Most theologians would insist on its being an unexaminable assumption indeed.

****

These Are a Few of My Favorite Things:
Lust
Gluttony
Envy
Anger
Greed
Sloth
Pride

\*\*\*\*

April 12, 2007.
Zucchini planted, in pots indoors, to be moved outside on May 1.

This year in the fruit trees I'll try something new. Traps for coddling moths. Last year coddling moths came to live in at least half of our apples, so that every bite was an investigative exercise and we couldn't, without admonitions, give them away to people. These commercial moth traps are designed like cardboard origami boxes, which you hang from a branch. They announce their brand-name in stylish letters on their side panels, "*Tanglefoot*." Pheromones seduce the moths inside, where, with their libido, they presumably die of impatience, hung up in the perfect breezes of May and June.

Personally, I've never minded eating an apple where a worm has lived. It only takes a little paying attention.

Plus, the worm isn't there anymore. It's just the tunnel he left behind in escaping. And I wouldn't be surprised if one of those caterpillers, born innocent inside an apple, is cleaner and more bacteria free than a human mouth.

The weather this spring was perfect throughout blossom time. Every petal and pistil has stayed intact, during a loud bee time. Already the pears are starting to look abundant. Knobs as big as marbles have appeared overnight, two or three for every foot of branch. I suppose culling will be in order. One particularly stupendous old tree seems to produce a full *unculled* crop of pears as big as softballs. When the August nights come, the sound of branches snapping will come over the meadow. A real farmer, I know, would fashion crutches for the branches. It's wasteful not to. (I've also seen slings, of torn bedsheets knotted.)

\*\*\*\*

The Power/Love Trade-Off. In the journey of forking paths (Is not

Life a Garden of Forking Paths?), at every fork, Love lies on one side, Power on the other. When you choose the one, you are forsaking the other. Also in choosing the one, you veer permanently farther from the other, as you go along.

(I notice this to be a constant theme in my fiction.)

****

May 17, 2007.

Hot days are here, and laundry is drying on the line. The rumble of the dryer, its jets of hot propane, will be idle for the summer mostly. Thanks to Al Gore, maybe now at last, rough-nap stiff bathtowels, folded on linen shelves, can be the *pride* of a clever household. Let them be a status symbol. Along with organic gardens, on the lawns of Winnetka, the redwood decks of Sausalito. Let Michelle Obama establish, beside her First organic garden on the White House lawn, the First clothesline, where the First boxer shorts may wave in the breeze.

The sight of laundry on a line today has caught me unawares in a sentimentality. We're educated to see really magnificent or summary beauty in certain conventional places—the Sistine Chapel, Bach's B-minor Mass, Proust's big book, the Grand Canyon, even a close look at a wildflower. I'm a conventionally educated man and I've been, of course, made aware of all the usual ways we're supposed to get access to "the sublime." But the sublime can sneak up from unexpected directions, and laundry on a line in the spring wind—the big bedsheets in various colors bellying out—comes to me now. There was a children's book we used to read to Hunter, called *All the Secrets of the World*, and it contained, spread out over two pages, a particularly moving illustration of a lawnful of laundry hanging out to dry, as seen through the eyes of a child. In a wind that was palpable from the artist's pastel strokes, on a slope of lawn that tilted with a moody passion and a predestined ineluctability, the great flying badges of laundry were framed to represent a scene a child would remember forever, a simple spring day, to one side a granny figure, slouched in her metal garden chair. Today on the meadow behind our mudroom, filtered through my memory of that artist's illustration, our laundry stretching from a pear tree's branch to the corner of the house above a cord of firewood—more than taking another crack at Proust, more than a day at the Louvre—exactly captures the thing I might come back for, if there were such a thing as "reincarnation." I would *leave* the Louvre, for this: I would walk right out of the rooms of Dutch masters and down the staircase, and get on a plane straight back here to this meadow. The pure and austere "sublime," according to my education, is *contaminated* by such corny ingredients as a particular sentimentality, and in this case, the taint of nostalgia, too. But an education isn't always and unfailingly a useful preparation for life. The whole *organism* is constituted for the perception of the elusive "truth-and-beauty" revelation.

****

I'm Elmer Fudd now. I'm Mr. MacGregor. A rabbit is my nemesis. He has dined systematically on my rows of broccoli, eschewing the lettuce and onions and the new asparagus-mist above the ground and Swiss chard. (The Swiss chard is, instead, food for green finches, and is a total loss.) So today I fortified the enclosure with finer-mesh wire, and I put a second latch on the garden gate at ankle-height, because a greedy rabbit can flow through the gap there. Will I soon be waiting at a rabbit hole with a big mallet up-raised?

****

Interesting. Fencing wire at Ridge Feed and Supply is gauged according to the size of the varmint it forfends: "gopher wire," "rabbit wire," "hog wire," etc.

****

June 10, 2007.
Broccoli has been mostly lost to the rabbit: two whole rows were nibbled down to nothing, in as many weeks. Now I've put finer-mesh wire all around, and all raids of the rabbit have come to an end.

Then this week, a quick hail storm put bullet holes in all the broad, soft leaves—pumpkin, zucchini, pepper, tomato. We were inside drinking wine with Oakley and Barbara. Had to run out in the dark, to (inspiration of the moment) pull molded-plastic chairs off their stacks and set them over the sprouts. The survivors are the corn, the onions, the cabbage, some of the lettuce that hasn't bolted, and about half the tomatoes.

\*\*\*\*

Good Meadow Party this year. *Three* fiddle players, with all the courtesy of the eminent, were here among the usual mix of dobros and guitars at the campfire. Also a great mandolin player.

\*\*\*\*

June 12, 2007.
I've been making a practice, for some years now, of sitting in the rear pews Sunday mornings at a very traditional Episcopalian church. It's fascinating, it's intellectually stimulating, and when I can manage it, it's an hour in the week well spent. Now I'm asked whether I "believe" in "all that."

It's an ineffectively framed question—the usual purely semantic trap—because "belief" is a word nobody has a handle on. The truth is, people don't know what they "believe." Rather, refer not to "beliefs" but refer to "things we say."

Of the "things we say," a few might be "beliefs" but the rest are just "announcements." And they're announcements for our own hearing, our own ears, our own enchantment. Especially when we talk of higher things—guardian angels, quarks—our one most-enchanted listener is ourselves.

An example of something we seem to *believe*, freely, is that this table here is solid and will support an elbow. Or, we *believe* that the light pouring into our eyes begins somewhere, and represents an object.

Or, we *believe* that, at the lapse of one moment, another moment will rush in, consecutively, to sustain the "flow" of "time." Those are things we *believe*. Call that theology.

★★★★

Flannery O'Connor, when asked whether she "believed in all that," said something like, Well, if it were all just a lot of symbolism, then the hell with it.

★★★★

The logic of Western religion: If you paint a slash of lamb's blood on your doorpost, the bully will pass by your house. The message is: "Pass me over. This house has *been* ruined. The one thing most precious here has already *been* slaughtered. Pass on by." Then X-ianity came along and did accomplish the slaughter of the son, quite publicly. [So purportedly "the game is up."]

★★★★

I was in L.A. on Saturday, at ten o'clock in the morning, giving a commencement speech to graduating students who had won awards for creative writing (I spent much of the time warning them basically not to be writers if they can possibly help it). Meanwhile Brett and Hunter were home on the meadow, in canvas chairs, watching baby birds learn to fly. According to Brett, they would zip out from the apple tree about fifteen feet, do a U-turn, and zip back into the tree.

★★★★

Other evidence of the season. Hunter on June 22 will get on a plane for New Hampshire. It's something I find myself boasting about. On the strength of a couple of string quartets, he has been accepted at a summer composers' school and been given a scholarship, so for six weeks he'll be gone from home for the first extended time. At the airport, he will enter that telescoping tube connecting airport to plane. He's sixteen. His parents will be shrinking at one end behind him waving bye, and he'll go through the plane hatch alone, carrying his ticket in hand, and start looking for his seat alone. What a great pleasure that moment is, for him.

\*\*\*\*

Don Knotts. Remember him? He was "Barney Fife" in the television show about the sleepy small-town sheriff. The protrusion of Adam's apple and eyeballs, the barfy mouth.

He has been on my mind lately. When I was young, Don Knotts was, to me, an excruciating instance of pitiable mistakenness. He was a man who had built a life upon his own ridiculousness, his scrawniness and foolishness, all to make people laugh. Compare him with Mick Jagger, who was incarnated in the exact same physical form as Don Knotts (fact: they were twins separated at birth) but Mick Jagger parlayed it into a form of power and glamour. When I was young Mick Jaggers's seemed a life much better spent.

\*\*\*\*

It's been a big year for wildlife. Big animal populations. As in no other summer, squirrels keep invading the Annex, taking bites from the apples in the fruitbowl. Neat black defecation-pellets by the phone and message machine. So we set a Have-a-Heart trap and release them by the Truckee River. Then as more squirrels appear, to be trapped and released, we begin to suspect that, Heffalump-like, it's the same squirrel over and over again, and not a multitude. It's suggested that, for identification purposes, we should spray paint this squirrel before releasing him again, and see if he turns up (as there is a Krylon spray can of "Champagne Gold" in the basement); but this idea is discarded because the other squirrels around the Truckee River might "gang up on" a new squirrel who showed up with too dangerous a fashion sense, wearing Champagne Gold.

And the bears. At lower elevations, this year, they're raiding my pear and apple trees. They leave huge piles of wet shit directly under the trees where they stand while sweeping lower branches of all their fruit.

At higher elevations in Squaw, they provide an instance of the Law of Unintended Consequences.

Here is that chain of events: For years the local bears learned to dine on people's garbage. Then, in order not to train up "Bad Bears," the new local law was that all garbage must be housed in bear-proof steel containers. Everybody invested in those, including poured-concrete footings. The result is that now bears, disappointed with garbage-forage, are entering houses freely and browsing around, hankering, gross, mystical. They need to be chased out by a feather-less biped waving his arms and hooting.

****

An unusually cold December. The compost heap outside in the mornings (last night's asparagus stem, banana peel, coffee grounds) is frozen sparkling. But still a little bit of summer hangs around: beside the kitchen sink, every time I lift the lid on the sloppy com-post bucket, one little fruit fly appears.

(It isn't the same fruit fly of course, it's a descendent and heir of the fruit fly I saw the day before. September's fruit fly seems to have reached a reproduction rate of exactly "replacement level" in there, months after his tribe's proper season.)

****

The form "Total Ecological Collapse" will take: It won't be a dra-matic crisis; simply an economic pinch will educate us. The price of an apple. The necessity to learn a new trade.

An Ohio U-Haul on I-80, driven by a hopeful fellow with his family. (Or of course perhaps a disappointed fellow). That's the "recession" for you. That's ecology.

And the art of making things last; which provides a pleasurable kind of creativity and a constant education. All I learned in grad-school is irrelevant. Our streets and roads could one day look like

Havana's, with old cars nicely maintained.

My ergonomic "BalanceBall" chair (a pilates ball on a pedestal with no backrest) has a puncture in the inflated sphere, so now it's patched with a bike inner-tube patch. Years ago I'd have ordered a new ball and spent forty dollars. This is how Ecological Collapse is starting to look, at least from here.

* * * *

"Cynic" in literature: one who sustains a display of eternal innocent wonderment at the portion of "evil" in the world which *he* is so uninquely sharp-eyed as to discern. It's a manner of evading looking within oneself to discover one's own portion. So, as literature, it's not really, anymore, for grown-ups. Good for kids. Samuel Clemens (Twain) would be an American instance. It's why so many of Twain's books are in the end tiresome, his always holding his own "Having Never Grown Up" before himself as a lamp to light the world. The world doesn't measure up, for him. Sorry, but Mr. Vonnegut is probably an example too. Very Twain-like. When I was young, his books got me interested in the moral power of fiction. A fond goodbye to Mr. Vonnegut. In heaven now with Barney Fife.

* * * *

January 4.
Hurricane-force winds are coming to the foothills. The National Weather Service radar shows a fantastic low-pressure zone offshore swirling, wandering our way. Have garaged both cars, set stones around the skirts of all my woodpile tarps, roped the loose-swinging gate, latched the screen doors by hook and eye from within, filled the bathtub with cold water (as our only cistern when the power goes out and the pump doesn't work).

* * * *

Winter: chain saw won't start and needs servicing; the lettuce has stopped growing and its leaves are hard and unappetizing; the woodpile is shrinking faster than I'd planned; Hunter is doing homeschooling this year and drinks coffee continually; all of us in pajamas at noon; no word from my agent.

✴✴✴✴

Poor old San Francisco. Now, there, one feels as if trapped inside a J. Peterman catalogue. ("Here's a devastating trench coat, as laconic as Bogie in *Casablanca*, as wounded as James Dean in *Rebel*. Oh, and here's a little café straight out of the Summer of Love. And in this little coffee shop for an afternoon, you can go back and be a beatnik again. Here's Buddhism, complete with black cloth shoes, here's Suffering Art, here's epicureanism, here's alienated mutilated sub-culture.") It's inevitable in pop culture, that the soul be trivialized, but SF used to be a small town and a provincial place, more isolated from the Great Marketplace of the Self. (Its reputation notwith-standing!) Indeed wasn't every place, once, more provincial?

(Kierkegaard, yes: The only real religion is solitude. [Implying that, where "any two are gathered in my name," it's already poppycock.])

Even much of the literature of our time has turned to a form of paraphrase and sly quotedness, J. Peterman catalogue style, where, under the guise of postmodernism, it succeeds as a series of clipped-together cliché attitudes. The Reign of Irony. Sometimes I think the appeal of irony, for the practitioner, is that it can sustain the feeling that he's immortal and never grows old, and stays beau-tiful, by never committing to any sincerity. Sincerity is death. When my son's pop music employs a "banjo" sound, it's only the *idea* of "a banjo," it's merely a quoted banjo, an ironic banjo, not the actual thing. An actual banjo, that would be a horror.

All I can suggest, at least for an artist, is, in the end, you have to love something.

✴✴✴✴

[Possibly even a sampled banjo.] [A banjo all made of diode oscilla-tions.]

****

May 1.

The mower's "blade deck" whacked against a fence post and is off-kilter. And all the belts need replacing. Fixing it is beyond my powers. I've been lying under it in the grass all morning. "Pearson Small Engine" in Grass Valley asks a fifty dollar pick-up and drop-off fee, to send out a trailer for it.

****

June.

Have delayed all plantings, especially of corn, in order to make fruit last longer into the fall. At this point, in the small garden patch, all I've done is turn over the soil.

# *Open City* Index (Issues 1–27)

Abreu, Jean Claude and Jorge Jauregui, trans., "The First Visit to the Louvre: Fragments of an Improbable Dialogue" (story) by Rafael Fernández de Villa-Urrutia. *Open City* 16 (2002–2003): 177–181.

Acconci, Vito. Three poems. *Open City* 5 (1997): 99–102.

Adams, Bill. "Interior, Exterior, Portrait, Still-Life, Landscape" (drawings). *Open City* 19 (2004): 73–83.

Alcalá, Rosa, trans., "The Brilliance of Orifices," "Mother of Pearl," "The Anatomy of Paper" (poems) by Cecilia Vicuña. *Open City* 14 (2001–2002): 151–154.

Alcalay, Ammiel, trans., "Hotel," "Precautionary Manifesto" (poems) by Semezdin Mehmedinovic. *Open City* 17 (2003): 141–142.

Alcalay, Henry. "Learn to Drive Trucks    Big Money" (story). *Open City* 26 (2008–2009): 81–100.

Ali, Mohammed Naseehu. "The Long Ride Back Home" (story). *Open City* 26 (2008–2009): 1–14.

Allen, Roberta. "Surreal" (story). *Open City* 9 (1999): 53–54.

Altmann, Howard. "Stones," "Gymnast in the Dark," "Island," "Sunday Monday" (poems). *Open City* 25: 177–182.

Alvaraz, A. Two Untitled Poems. *Open City* 3 (1995): 72–74.

Ames, Greg. "Physical Discipline" (story). *Open City* 17 (2003): 209–216.

Ames, Jonathan. "Writer for Hire: A Spencer Johns Story" (story). *Open City* 9 (1999): 55–68.

Ames, Jonathan. "I Was in Flowers" (story). *Open City* 25 (2008): 39–44.

Anderson, Jack. "Elsewhere," "Believing in Ghosts" (poems). *Open City* 19 (2004): 51–53.

Anderson, Lucy. "Another Fish Poem" (poem). *Open City* 4 (1996): 195–196.

Andoe, Joe. "This Would Be the Day All My Dreams Come True," "Fence," "Seeing Red," "Eighteen-Year-Old Stucco Laborer and White Crosses" (poems). *Open City* 16 (2002–2003): 59–62.

Anderson, Lucy. "Winter Solstice," "Reentry," "What If, Then Nothing" (poems). *Open City* 9 (1999): 141–144.

Antoniadis, Tony. "Rescue 907!" (story). *Open City* 20 (2005): 181–193.

Arnold, Craig. "SSSSSSHHHHHH," "There is a circle drawn around you," "Your friend's arriving on the bus" (poems). *Open City* 16 (2002–2003): 97–105.

Badanes, Jerome. "Change Or Die" (unfinished novel). *Open City* 5 (1997): 159–233.

Badanes, Jerome. "The Man in the Twelve Thousand Rooms" (essay). *Open City* 23 (2007): 1–3.

Badanes, Jerome. "Guinea Golden," "From Day to Day," "Late Night Footsteps on the Staircase" (poems). *Open City* 23 (2007): 5–10.

Bakowski, Peter. "The Width of the World," "We Are So Rarely Out of the Line of Fire" (poems). *Open City* 11 (2000): 95–100.

Balkenhol, Stephan. Drawings. *Open City* 5 (1997): 38–42.

Bar-Nadav, Hadara. "Talking to Strangers" (story). *Open City* 23 (2007): 11–23.

Bar-Nadav, Hadara. "Bricolage and Blood," "I Used to Be Snow White," "To Halve and to Hole" (poems). *Open City* 23 (2007): 25–29.

Bartók-Baratta, Edward. "Walker" (poem). *Open City* 18 (2003–2004): 175.

Batlle, Jay. "People Like This Hate People Like You" (drawings). *Open City* 24 (2007–2008): 119–124.

Baum, Erica. "The Following Information" (photographs). *Open City* 13 (2001): 87–94.

Baumbach, Jonathan. "Lost Car" (story). *Open City* 22 (2006): 27–35.

Baumbach, Jonathan. "Travels with Wizard" (story) *Open City* 24 (2007–2008): 125–136.

Baumbach, Nico. "Guilty Pleasure" (story). *Open City* 14 (2001–2002): 39–58.

Beal, Daphne. "Eternal Bliss" (story). *Open City* 12 (2001): 171–190.

Beatty, Paul. "All Aboard" (poem). *Open City* 3 (1995): 245–247.

Becker, Priscilla. "Blue Statuary," "Instrumental" (poems). *Open City* 18 (2003–2004): 151–152.

Becker, Priscilla. "Recurrence of Childhood Paralysis," "Blue Statuary" (poems). *Open City* 19 (2004): 33–34.

Becker, Priscilla. "Typochondria" (essay). *Open City* 22 (2006): 9–12.

Becker, Priscilla. "Math Poem," "Midwestern," "afters," "Desert," "Hatred of Men with Blonde Eyebrows" (poems). *Open City* 26 (2008–2009): 15–20.

Beckman, Joshua and Tomaž Šalamun, trans., "VI," "VII" (poems) by Tomaž Šalamun. *Open City* 15 (2002): 155–157.

Beckman, Joshua and Tomaž Šalamun, trans.,"Porcini," "Spring Street" (poems) by Tomaž Šalamun. *Open City* 27 (2009):147–150 .

Beckman, Joshua and Matthew Rohrer. "Still Life with Woodpecker," "The Book of Houseplants" (poems). *Open City* 19 (2004): 177–178.

Belcourt, Louise. "Snake, World Drawings" (drawings). *Open City* 14 (2001–2002): 59–67.

Bellamy, Dodie. "From *Cunt-Ups*" (poems). *Open City* 14 (2001–2002): 155–157.

Beller, Thomas. "Vas *Is* Dat?" (story). *Open City* 10 (2000): 51–88.

Bellows, Nathaniel. "At the House on the Lake," "A Certain Dirge," "An Attempt" (poems). *Open City* 16 (2002–2003): 69–73.

Benton, William. "Midnight," "The Tin Room," "Saltwater," "Science" (poems). *Open City* 26 (2008–2009): 53–57.

Bergman, Alicia. "Visit" (story). *Open City* 10 (2000): 125–134.

Berman, David. "Snow," "Moon" (poems). *Open City* 4 (1996): 45–48.

Berman, David. "Classic Water & Other Poems" (poems). *Open City* 5 (1997): 21–26.

Berman, David. "Now, II," "A Letter From Isaac Asimov to His Wife, Janet, Written on His Deathbed" (poems). *Open City* 7 (1999): 56–59.

Bridges, Margaret Park. "Looking Out" (story). *Open City* 6 (1998): 47–59.

Broun, Bill. "Heart Machine Time" (story). *Open City* 11 (2000): 111–118.

Brown, Erin. "Reckoning" (story). *Open City* 24 (2007–2008): 99–102.

Bao, Quang. "Date" (poem). *Open City* 8 (1999): 137–140.

Brown, Jason. "North" (story). *Open City* 19 (2004): 1–19.

Brown, Lee Ann. "Discalmer" (introduction). *Open City* 14 (2001–2002): 137–139.

Brownstein, Michael. "The Art of Diplomacy" (story). *Open City* 4 (1996): 153–161.

Brownstein, Michael. "From *World on Fire*" (poetry). *Open City* 14 (2001–2002): 201–218.

Broyard, Bliss. "Snowed In" (story). *Open City* 7 (1999): 22–42.

Brumbaugh, Sam. "Safari Eyes" (story). *Open City* 12 (2001): 49–64.

Bukowski, Charles. "The Silver Christ of Santa Fe" (story). *Open City* 25 (2008): 63–68.

Bunn, David. "Book Worms" (card catalog art project). *Open City* 16 (2002–2003): 43–57.

Burton, Jeff. "Untitled #87 (chandelier)" (photograph). *Open City* 7 (1999): front cover.

Butler, Robert Olen. "Three Pieces of *Severance*" (stories). *Open City* 19 (2004): 189–191.

C, Mark. "What Calls Your Name" (photographs). *Open City* 25 (2008): 137–146.

Carter, Emily. "Glory Goes and Gets Some" (story). *Open City* 4 (1996): 125–128.

Carter, Emily. "Hampden City" (story). *Open City* 7 (1999): 43–45.

Cattelan, Maurizio. "Choose Your Destination, Have a Museum-Paid Vacation" (postcard). *Open City* 9 (1999): 39–42.

Cavendish, Lucy. "Portrait of an Artist's Studio" (drawings). *Open City* 11 (2000): 101–110.

Chamandy, Susan. "Hannibal Had Elephants with Him" (story). *Open City* 18 (2003–2004): 33–54.

Chan, Paul. "Self-Portrait as a Font" (drawings, text). *Open City* 15 (2002): 111–118.

Chancellor, Alexander. "The Special Relationship" (story). *Open City* 9 (1999): 189–206.

Charles, Bryan. "Dollar Movies" (story). *Open City* 19 (2004): 41–49.

Charles, Bryan. "There's a Road to Everywhere Except Where You Came From" (story). *Open City* 27 (2009): 87–110.

Chase, Heather. "My First Facelift" (story). *Open City* 4 (1996): 23–44.

Chester, Alfred. "Moroccan Letters" (story). *Open City* 3 (1995): 195–219.

Chester, Craig. "Why the Long Face?" (story). *Open City* 14 (2001–2002): 109–127.

Chung, Brian Carey. "Still Life," "Traveling with the Lost" (poems). *Open City* 21 (2005–2006): 1153–156.

Clark, Joseph. "Nature Freak" (story). *Open City* 21 (2005–2006): 121–130.

Clements, Marcelle. "Reliable Alchemy" (story). *Open City* 17 (2003): 239–241.

Cohen, Elizabeth. "X-Ray of My Spine" (poem). *Open City* 2 (1993): 61–62.

Dietrich, Bryan D. "This Island Earth" (poem). *Open City* 16 (2002–2003): 201–202.

Dietrich, Bryan D. "The Thing That Couldn't Die" (poem). *Open City* 21 (2005–2006): 89–90.

Dikeou, Devon. Photographs, drawings, and text. *Open City* 1 (1992): 39–48.

Dikeou, Devon. "Marilyn Monroe Wanted to Be Buried In Pucci" (photographs, drawings, text, ). *Open City* 10 (2000): 207–224.

Donnelly, Mary. "Lonely" (poem). *Open City* 12 (2001): 151–152.

Doris, Stacy. "Flight" (play). *Open City* 14 (2001–2002): 147–150.

Dormen, Lesley. "Gladiators" (story). *Open City* 18 (2003–2004): 155–163.

Douglas, Norman. "Male Order" (story). *Open City* 19 (2004): 151–163.

Dowe, Tom. "Legitimation Crisis" (poem). *Open City* 7 (1999): 21.

Doyle, Ben. "And on the First Day" (poem). *Open City* 12 (2001): 203–204.

Duhamel, Denise. "The Frog and the Feather" (story). *Open City* 5 (1997): 115–117.

Dyer, Geoff. "Albert Camus" (story). *Open City* 9 (1999): 23–38.

Grennan, Eamon. "Two Poems" (poems). *Open City* 5 (1997): 137–140.

Eisenegger, Erich. "A Ticket for Kat" (story). *Open City* 16 (2002–2003): 133–141.

Ellison, Lori. "Coffee Drawings" (drawings). *Open City* 13 (2001): 57–66.

Ellison, Lori. Drawing. *Open City* 17 (2003): back cover.

Ellman, Juliana. "Interior, Exterior, Portrait, Still-Life, Landscape" (drawings). *Open City* 19 (2004): 73–83.

Elsayed, Dahlia. "Black and Blue" (story). *Open City* 2 (1993): 29–35.

Elsayed, Dahlia. "Paterson Falls" (story). *Open City* 9 (1999): 153–158.

Engel, Terry. "Sky Blue Ford" (story). *Open City* 3 (1995): 115–128.

Eno, Will. "The Short Story of My Family" (story). *Open City* 13 (2001): 79–86.

Epstein, Daniel Mark. "The Jealous Man" (poem). *Open City* 17 (2003): 135–136.

Erian, Alicia. "Troika" (story). *Open City* 15 (2002): 27–42.

Erian, Alicia. "The Grant" (story). *Open City* 19 (2004): 109–117.

Eurydice. "History Malfunctions" (story). *Open City* 3 (1995): 161–164.

Evans, CJ. "Today You Will Not Die a Horrible Death," "Him Can We Save"(poems). *Open City* 27 (2009): 35–36.

Faison, Ann. Drawings. *Open City* 12 (2001): 197–202.

Fandel, John. "Picture Postcard," "Spanish Lessons," "Snowing and Knowing," "Mused" (poems). *Open City* 26 (2008–2009): 101–106.

Fattaruso, Paul. "Breakfast," "It Is I," "On the Stroke and Death of My Grandfather" (poems). *Open City* 20 (2005): 217–221.

Fawkes, Martin, trans., "Rehearsal for a Deserted City" (story) by Giuseppe O. Longo. *Open City* 15 (2002): 95–103.

Fernández de Villa-Urrutia, Rafael. "The First Visit to the Louvre: Fragments of an Improbable Dialogue" (story), trans. Jean Claude Abreu and Jorge Jauregui. *Open City* 16 (2002–2003): 177–181.

Field, Edward. Epilogue for Alfred Chester's "Moroccan Letters." *Open City* 3 (1995): 219.

Gillison, Samantha. "Petty Cash" (story). *Open City* 4 (1996): 197–206.

Ginsberg, Allen. Photograph and text. *Open City* 3 (1995): 191–194.

Gizzi, Peter. "Take the 5:01 to Dreamland" (poem). *Open City* 17 (2003): 151–152.

Gold, Herbert. "Next In Line" (story). *Open City* 22 (2006): 65–69.

Goldstein, Jesse. "Dance With Me Ish, Like When You Was a Baby" (story). *Open City* 17 (2003): 197–199.

Golliver, Benjamin. "Las Vegas Bypass" (essay). *Open City* 26 (2008–2009): 121–130.

Gonzales, Mark. "To You, My Reader" (story). *Open City* 8 (1999): 153–154.

Gonzalez, Manuel. "The Disappearance of the Sebali Tribe" (story). *Open City* 22 (2006): 49–64.

Gonzalez, Wayne. "Interior, Exterior, Portrait, Still-Life, Landscape," "The Carousel Club," "Self-Portrait as a Young Marine" (paintings). *Open City* 19 (2004): 73–83; front and back covers.

Gooch, Brad. "Flannery at Iowa" (nonfiction). *Open City* 26 (2008–2009): 135–162.

Goodyear, Dana. "Things Get Better Before They Get Worse," "Oracle," "Séance at Tennis," "Setting" (poems). *Open City* 16 (2002–2003): 39–42.

Gorham, Sarah. "Bacchus at the Water Tower, Continuing Ed," "Middle Age" (poems). *Open City* 13 (2001): 111–114.

Gorham, Sarah. "The Sacrifice," "*Would you like to see the house?*" (poems). *Open City* 19 (2004): 119–121.

Gray, Peter. "Alley" (poem). *Open City* 16 (2002–2003): 183–184.

Green, Karen. "Damaging Enactments" (art project). *Open City* 27 (2009): 77–86.

Green, Karen. "Mrs. John White Alexander" and "Oak" (mixed media). *Open City* 27 (2009): front and back covers.

Green, Lohren. "From the *Poetical Dictionary*" (poem). *Open City* 16 (2002–2003): 129–132.

Greene, Daniel. "Paul's Universe Blue," "Mother, Worcester, 1953," "Learning to Stand" (poems). *Open City* 15 (2002): 43–47.

Grennan, Eamon. "Glimpse" (poem). *Open City* 17 (2003): 161.

Groebner, John. "The Fucker" (story). *Open City* 25 (2008): 161–168.

Grove, Elizabeth. "Enough About Me" (story). *Open City* 14 (2001–2002): 97–108.

Gunn, Kirsty. "Dick" (story). *Open City* 26 (2008–2009): 21–24.

Hakansson, Henrik. "Incomplete Proposals 1999–" (drawings). *Open City* 12 (2001): 89–94.

Hall, Kate. "Remind Me What the Light Is For" (poem). *Open City* 24 (2007–2008): 33–34.

Hall, Marcellus. "As Luke Would Have It" (drawings, text). *Open City* 18 (2003–2004): 177–184.

Hannah, Duncan. Drawings. *Open City* 25 (2008): 169–176 and back cover.

Hannah, Duncan. "High Diver" (painting). *Open City* 25 (2008): front cover.

Hannaham, James. "Loss Prevention" (story). *Open City* 24 (2007–2008): 15–32.

Hanrahan, Catherine. "The Outer-Space Room" (story). *Open City* 18 (2003-2004): 99–114.

Hofstede, Hilarius. "The Marquis Von Water" (text art project). *Open City* 3 (1995): 135–144.

Hogan, John Brinton. "Vacation" (photographs). *Open City* 20 (2005): 113–120.

Holland, J. Gill. Introduction to "The Journals of Edvard Munch." *Open City* 9 (1999): 229–232.

Holland, Noy. "Time for the Flat-Headed Man" (story). *Open City* 14 (2001–2002): 69–80.

Hollander, Katherine. "Snow Man" (poem). *Open City* 19 (2004): 187–188.

Homes, A. M. "Do You Hear What I Hear?" (story). *Open City* 27 (2009): 63–76.

Howe, Fanny. "The Plan," "A Reach" (poems). *Open City* 17 (2003): 119–121.

Humphries, Jacqueline. Paintings. *Open City* 3 (1995): 235–244.

Hubby, Bettina. Illustrations for Susan Perry's "The Final Man." *Open City* 8 (1999): 15–171.

Iovenko, Chris. "The Turnaround" (story). *Open City* 5 (1997): 73–80.

Jack, Rodney. "Many Splendid Thing," "Mutually Exclusive" (poems). *Open City* 18 (2003–2004): 61–66.

Jack, Rodney. "From Nightlife" (story). *Open City* 23 (2007): 97–110.

Jack, Rodney. "Seedbed," "Black-Capped Chickadee Trapped in the Feeder," "Perpetuation" (poems). *Open City* 23 (2007): 111–114.

Jaicks, David. "Grocery Store" (poem). *Open City* 27 (2009): 111–112.

Jaramillo, Luis. "Jack and the Rotarians" (story). *Open City* 19 (2004): 85–91.

Jarnot, Lisa. "Self-Portrait" (poem). *Open City* 14 (2001–2002): 167.

Jauregui, Jorge and Jean Claude Abreu, trans., "The First Visit to the Louvre: Fragments of an Improbable Dialogue" (story) by Rafael Fernández de Villa-Urrutia. *Open City* 16 (2002–2003): 177–181.

John, Daniel. "The Diagnosis" (poem). *Open City* 19 (2004): 93.

Johnson, David. Image and text. *Open City* 3 (1995): 155–160.

Johnson, Denis. "An Anarchist's Guide to Somalia" (story). *Open City* 4 (1996): 89–116.

Johnson, Jeff. "The Breather" (story). *Open City* 24 (2007–2008): 1–14.

Johnson, Joyce. "Postwar" (story). *Open City* 8 (1999): 183–194.

Johnson, Marilyn A. "Her Deflowering" (poem). *Open City* 16 (2002–2003): 191.

Johnston, Bret Anthony. "Waterwalkers" (story). *Open City* 18 (2003–2004): 229–248.

Jones, Hettie. "5:15 p.m. Eastern Standard Time, November," "One Hundred Love Poems for Lisa" (poems). *Open City* 4 (1996): 86–88.

Jones, Sarah. "Dining Room (Francis Place) (III)" (photograph, detail). *Open City* 5 (1997): front cover.

Jones, Stephen Graham. "Bile" (story). *Open City* 14 (2001–2002): 81–88.

Kang, Christopher. "The Anarchist Thinks of Winter," "The Cy Twombly Poem" (poems). *Open City* 26 (2008–2009): 115–120.

Kaplan, Janet. "The List" (poem). *Open City* 19 (2004): 71.

Kay, Hellin. "Moscow & New York, Coming & Going" (photographs, story). *Open City* 15 (2002): 81–92.

Kronovet, Jennifer. "Recipient," "A Self-Guided Tour," "Together" (poems). *Open City* 26 (2008–2009): 131–134.

Kujak, Heidi. "Father's Day," "San Francisco Produce Terminal" (poems). *Open City* 15 (2002): 109–110.

Labbe, Jason. "(text message)," "(depth of field)" from "Dear Photographer" (poems). *Open City* 27 (2009): 51–52.

Lamb-Shapiro, Jessica. "This Man Is Eating in His Sleep" (story). *Open City* 17 (2003): 167–175.

Lambert, Alix. Untitled photographs. *Open City* 3 (1995): front cover and 34.

Lambert, Alix. "The Mark of Cain" (photographs, text). *Open City* 10 (2000): 183–194.

Lambert, Alix. "I am not like them at all and I cannot pretend" (collage). *Open City* 18 (2003–2004): 81–86.

Larimer, Heather. "Casseroles" (story). *Open City* 12 (2001): 75–88.

Larkin, Joan. "Full Moon Over Brooklyn" (poem). *Open City* 17 (2003): 123.

Larralde, Martin G. Paintings. *Open City* 11 (2000): 87–94.

Larson, Laura and Anne Trubek. "Genius Loci" (photographs, text). *Open City* 7 (1999): 85–94.

Larsson, Victoria. "Sharp Objects" (story). *Open City* 18 (2003–2004): 167–173.

Lasdun, James. "The Natural Order" (story). *Open City* 15 (2002): 201–221.

Lazar, Zachary. "Meherangarh" (story) *Open City* 27 (2009): 37–46.

Lea, Creston. "We Used to Breed Remarkable Percheron Twitch Horses" (poem). *Open City* 12 (2001): 271.

Leckey, Mark. "The Casuals" (drawings, text). *Open City* 9 (1999): 119–128.

Leebron, Fred. "Welcome to Arcadia" (story). *Open City* 8 (1999): 111–119.

Legere, Phoebe. "Ode to Hong Kong" (poem). *Open City* 1 (1992): 23.

Lehman, David. "Eleven Poems for My Birthday" (poems). *Open City* 18 (2003–2004): 225–228.

Lehman, David. "Fast and Slow Sestina," "The Hotel Fiesta Sestina" (poems). *Open City* 20 (2005): 93–96.

LeMay, Patty. "confessions of a touring musician's lady (part 1)," "confessions of a touring musician's lady (part 24)" (poems). *Open City* 18 (2003–2004): 119–122.

Lemon, Alex. "Dourine," "Hallelujah Blackout" (poems). *Open City* 24 (2007–2008): 103–106.

Lesser, Guy. "The Good Sportsman, Et Cetera" (story). *Open City* 8 (1999): 75–86.

Levine, Margaret. "In a Dream It Happens," "Dilemma" (poems). *Open City* 16 (2002–2003): 159–160.

Lewinsky, Monica. "I Am a Pizza" (poem). *Open City* 6 (1998): 129.

Lewis, Jeremy. Introduction to "Happy Deathbeds." *Open City* 4 (1996): 49–52.

Lichtenstein, Miranda. "Stills from *The Naked City*" and "Untitled, #4 (Richardson Park)" (photographs). *Open City* 12 (2001): 275–284; front and back covers.

Lichtenstein, Miranda. "Ganzfeld" (photograph). *Open City* 21 (2005–2006): front and back covers.

Lida, David. "Bewitched" (story). *Open City* 9 (1999): 69–90.

Maxwell, Glyn. "Sufficient Time," "Reality," "Decision," "Dust and Flowers," "The Arms of Half," "Fall of Man [Continued]" (poems). *Open City* 23 (2007): 149–156.

Maxwell, Richard. "A–1 Rolling Steak House" (play). *Open City* 13 (2001): 181–187.

McCabe, Patrick. "The Call" (story). *Open City* 3 (1995): 95–103.

McCormick, Carlo. "The Getaway" (story, drawings). *Open City* 3 (1995): 151–154.

McCracken, Chad. "Postcolonial Fat Man," "Second Grade" (poems). *Open City* 19 (2004): 165–167.

McCurtin, William. "Sometimes Skateboarding Is Like Dancing with Criminals" (drawings). *Open City* 20 (2005): 201–208.

McGuane, Thomas. "Bees" (story). *Open City* 4 (1996): 215–222.

McIntyre, Vestal. "Octo" (story). *Open City* 11 (2000): 27–50.

McIntyre, Vestal. "The Trailer at the End of the Driveway" (essay). *Open City* 22 (2006): 1–7.

McIntyre, Vestal. "Late in Life" (story). *Open City* 27 (2009): 1–14.

McKenna, Evie. "Directions to My House" (photographs). *Open City* 12 (2001): 65–72.

McNally, John. "The First of Your Last Chances" (story). *Open City* 11 (2000): 125–140.

McNally, Sean. "Handsome Pants" (story). *Open City* 6 (1998): 131–132.

McPhee, Martha. "Waiting" (story). *Open City* 2 (1993): 109–118.

Mead, Stu. "Devil Milk" and "Untitled" (drawings). *Open City* 17 (2003): 177–185 and front cover.

Means, David. "What They Did" (story). *Open City* 6 (1998): 77–82.

Mehmedinovic, Semezdin. "Hotel Room," "Precautionary Manifesto" (poems), trans. Ammiel Alcaly. *Open City* 17 (2003): 141–142.

Mehta, Diane. "Rezoning in Brooklyn" (poem). *Open City* 7 (1999): 71–72.

Mendel, David, trans., "In Zenoburg" (story) by Giuseppe O. Longo. *Open City* 12 (2001): 153–160.

Mendel, David, trans., "Braised Beef for Three" (story) by Giuseppe O. Longo. *Open City* 19 (2004): 135–148.

Mengestu, Dinaw. "Home at Last" (essay). *Open City* 24 (2007–2008): 107–112.

Merlis, Jim. "One Man's Theory" (story). *Open City* 10 (2000): 171–182.

Metres, Philip and Tatiana Tulchinsky, trans., "This Is Me" (poem) by Lev Rubinshtein. *Open City* 15 (2002): 121–134.

Michels, James B., trans., "Conjectures about Hell" (story) by Giuseppe O. Longo. *Open City* 25 (2008): 183–190.

Michels, Victoria Kohn. "At the Nightingale-Bamford School for Girls" (poem). *Open City* 4 (1996): 166–167.

Middlebrook, Jason. "APL #1 Polar Bear" (drawing). *Open City* 18 (2003–2004): front and back covers.

Milford, Kate. Photographs. *Open City* 2 (1993): 54–56.

Milford, Matthew. "Civil Servants" (paintings, text). *Open City* 7 (1999): 47–55.

Miller, Greg. "Intercessor" (poem). *Open City* 11 (2000): 51.

Miller, Jane. "From *A Palace of Pearls*" (poem). *Open City* 17 (2003): 157–160.

Miller, Matt. "Driver" (poem). *Open City* 12 (2001): 169–170.

Miller, Matt. "Chimera" (poem). *Open City* 21 (2005–2006): 119–120.

Miller, Stephen Paul. "When Listening to the Eighteen-and-a-Half Minute Tape Gap as Electronic Music" (poem). *Open City* 4 (1996): 162.

M.I.M.E. Photographs. *Open City* 9 (1999): 207–218.

Mobilio, Albert. "Adhesiveness: There Was This Guy" (story). *Open City* 5 (1997): 55–56.

Moeckel, Thorpe. "Johnny Stinkbait Bears His Soul" (story). *Open City* 23 (2007): 157–162.

Moeckel, Thorpe. "Dream of My Father," "Nature Poem, Inc.," "Mussels," "At the Co-op," "Beautiful Jazz" (poems). *Open City* 23 (2007): 163–171.

Moody, Rick. "Dead Man Writes," "Domesticity," "Immortality," "Two Sonnets for Stacey" (poems). *Open City* 6 (1998): 83–88.

Moore, Honor. "She Remembers," "The Heron" (poems). *Open City* 13 (2001): 71–78.

Moore, Honor. "In Place of an Introduction" (assemblage). *Open City* 17 (2003): 105–106.

Moore, Honor. "Homage," "Hotel Brindisi," "Tango" (poems). *Open City* 20 (2005): 77–80.

Mortensen, Viggo. "From *Hole in the Sun*" (photographs). *Open City* 18 (2003–2004): 141–150.

Moss, Stanley. "Satyr Song" (memoir). *Open City* 24 (2007–2008): 137–145.

Mullen, Harryette. "Unacknowledged Legislator," "Headlines," "Bumper to Bumper" (poems). *Open City* 14 (2001–2002): 141–143.

Munch, Edvard. "Passages from the Journals of Edvard Munch" (text, drawings). *Open City* 9 (1999): 233–250.

Münch, Christopher. Photographs, text. *Open City* 3 (1995): 89–94.

Mycue, Edward. "But the Fifties Really Take Me Home" (poem). *Open City* 11 (2000): 171–172.

Nadin, Peter. Paintings. *Open City* 4 (1996): 147–152.

Myles, Eileen. "Ooh" (poem). *Open City* 17 (2003): 143.

Myles, Eileen. "The Inferno" (story). *Open City* 18 (2003–2004): 67–74.

Nachumi, Ben. "Spring Cabin," "Crows," "Viking (to Calculus I)," "Dream House" (poems). *Open City* 21 (2005–2006): 71–76.

Nakanishi, Nadine. "Seriidevüf" (drawings). *Open City* 19 (2004): 122–128.

Nelson, Cynthia. "go ahead and sing your weird arias," "the adoration piles of spring," "i almost get killed" (poems). *Open City* 14 (2001–2002): 169–171.

Nelson, Maggie. "The Poem I Was Working on Before September 11, 2001" (poem). *Open City* 14 (2001–2002): 179–183.

Nester, Daniel. "After Schubert's Sad Cycle of Songs" (poem). *Open City* 15 (2002): 165–168.

Nevers, Mark. "Untitled" (poem). *Open City* 20 (2005): 121.

Newirth, Mike. "Semiprecious" (story). *Open City* 18 (2003–2004): 87–96.

Nutt, David. "Melancholera" (story) *Open City* 21 (2005–2006): 53–69.

O'Brien, Geoffrey. "Roof Garden" (poem). *Open City* 3 (1995): 134.

O'Brien, Geoffrey. "The Blasphemers" (story). *Open City* 5 (1997): 43–54.

O'Brien, Geoffrey. "House Detective" (poem). *Open City* 8 (1999): 120.

O'Brien, Geoffrey. "The Browser's Ecstasy" (story). *Open City* 10 (2000): 195–202.

O'Connor, John. "The Boil" (story). *Open City* 25 (2008): 147–160.

O'Rourke, Meg. "The Drivers" (story). *Open City* 2 (1993): 93–96.

Ogger, Sara, trans., "Show #7" (story) by Benjamin von Stuckrad-Barre. *Open City* 12 (2001): 119–130.

Okubo, Michiko. "The Glass Garden" (story). *Open City* 14 (2001–2002): 33–38.

Oldham, Will. "Untitled" (poem). *Open City* 7 (1999): 78.

Ortiz, Radames. "The Plea" (poem). *Open City* 18 (2003–2004): 211–212.

Osborne, Lawrence. "Gentle Toys" (story). *Open City* 4 (1996): 186–194.

Ovaldé, Véronique. "Scenes from Family Life" (story), trans. Lorin Stein. *Open City* 21 (2005–2006): 141–152.

Owens, Laura. Drawings *Open City* 9 (1999): 145–152.

Paco. "Clown Speaks" (story). *Open City* 2 (1993): 77–81.

Paco. "Clown White" (story). *Open City* 3 (1995): 103–110.

Paco. "Ing," "Cross and Sundial," "Flares," (stories), "Firecrackers and Sneakers" (poem). *Open City* 9 (1999): 219–226.

Pagk, Paul. Drawings. *Open City* 5 (1997): 89–98.

Panurgias, Basile. "The Sixth Continent" (story). *Open City* 5 (1997): 81–89.

Pape, Eric. "Faces of the Past and the Future" (essay). *Open City* 22 (2006): 13–25.

Passaro, Vince. "Cathedral Parkway" (story). *Open City* 1 (1992): 26–34.

Passaro, Vince. "Adult Content" (story). *Open City* 13 (2001): 227–235.

Passaro, Vince. "Voluntary Tyranny, or Brezhnev at the Mall: Notes from Wartime on the Willful Abdication of the Liberty We Claim We're Busy Promoting Elsewhere" (essay). *Open City* 22 (2006): 39–56.

Patterson, G. E. "Drift Land" (poem). *Open City* 17 (2003): 137–138.

Pavlic, Ed. "You Sound Unseen" (poem). *Open City* 9 (1999): 227.

Pavlic, Ed. "From *Arachnida Speak*" (poem). *Open City* 16 (2002–2003): 155–157.

Pelevin, Victor. "Who By Fire" (story), trans. Matvei Yankelevich. *Open City* 7 (1999): 95–106.

Penone, Giuseppe. "Reversing One's Own Eyes" (photograph). *Open City* 9 (1999): 91–94.

Perry, Susan. "The Final Man" (story). *Open City* 8 (1999): 155–171.

Petrantoni, Lorenzo. "1880" (collages). *Open City* 21 (2005–2006): 21–28.

Phillips, Alex. "Stonemason's Oratory," "Work Shy," "Dressmaker" (poems). *Open City* 21 (2005–2006): 49–51.

Phillips, Robert. Introduction to "T. S. Eliot's Squint" by Delmore Schwartz. *Open City* 5 (1997): 152.

Pierson, Melissa Holbrook. "Night Flight" (poem). *Open City* 13 (2001): 131.

Pinchbeck, Daniel. "Fleck" (story). *Open City* 10 (2000): 239–272.

Rofihe, Rick and Thomas Robertson. "Four Round Windows" (drawings, text). *Open City* 19 (2004): 213–222.

Rohrer, Matthew and Joshua Beckman. "Still Life with Woodpecker," "The Book of Houseplants" (poems). *Open City* 19 (2004): 177–178.

Ross, Sally. "Interior, Exterior, Portrait, Still-Life, Landscape" (drawings). *Open City* 19 (2004): 73–83.

Rothman, Richard. "Photographs" (photographs). *Open City* 6 (1998): 116–124.

Rubinshtein, Lev. "This Is Me" (poem), trans. Philip Metres and Tatiana Tulchinsky. *Open City* 15 (2002): 121–134.

Rubinstein, Raphael, trans., "From *Letter to Antonio Saura*" (story) by Marcel Cohen. *Open City* 17 (2003): 217–225.

Ruda, Ed. "The Seer" (story). *Open City* 1 (1992): 15.

Ruppersberg, Allen. "Greetings from L.A." (novel). *Open City* 16 (2002–2003): throughout.

Rush, George. "Interior, Exterior, Portrait, Still-Life, Landscape" (print). *Open City* 19 (2004): 73–83.

Ruvo, Christopher. "Afternoon, 1885" (poem). *Open City* 18 (2003–2004): 185–186.

Rux, Carl Hancock. "Geneva Cottrell, Waiting for the Dog to Die" (play). *Open City* 13 (2001): 189–213.

Šalamun, Tomaž. "VI," "VII" (poems), trans. author and Joshua Beckman. *Open City* 15 (2002): 155–157.

Šalamun, Tomaž. "Porcini," "Spring Street" (poems), trans. author and Joshua Beckman. *Open City* 27 (2009):147–150.

Salmon, Audrey. "Mutant Architecture" (art project). *Open City* 27 (2009): 51–60.

Salvatore, Joseph. "Practice Problem" (story). *Open City* 7 (1999): 127–135.

Samore, Sam and Max Henry. "Hobo Deluxe, A Cinema of Poetry" (photographs and text). *Open City* 12 (2001): 257–270.

Samton, Matthew. "Y2K, or How I Learned to Stop Worrying and Love the CD-Rom" (poem). *Open City* 12 (2001): 191–196.

Saroyan, Strawberry. "Popcorn" (story). *Open City* 6 (1998): 125–128.

Saroyan, Strawberry. "Strawberry Is" (poem). *Open City* 26 (2008–2009): 73–80.

Sayrafiezadeh, Saïd. "My Mother and the Stranger" (story). *Open City* 17 (2003): 59–66.

Schaeffer, Doug. "Withdrawn" (collages). *Open City* 24 (2007–2008): 93–98 and back cover.

Schleinstein, Bruno. "Drawings" (drawings). *Open City* 17 (2003): 227–237.

Schles, Ken. Two untitled photographs. *Open City* 1 (1992): front and back covers.

Schles, Ken. Photography. *Open City* 2 (1993): front cover.

Schles, Ken. Two photographs. *Open City* 10 (2000): front and back covers.

Schles, Ken. "New York City: Street Photographs Following the Terrorist Attack on the World Trade Center, September 2001" (photographs). *Open City* 14 (2001–2002): 219–232.

Schmidt, Elizabeth. "Crossing Chilmark Pond," "Quiet Comfort" (poems). *Open City* 26 (2008–2009): 25–31.

Sledge, Michael. "The Birdlady of Houston" (story). *Open City* 16 (2002–2003): 211–221.

Smith, Charlie. "A Selection Process," "Agents of the Moving Company," "Evasive Action" (poems). *Open City* 6 (1998): 43–46.

Smith, Lee. Two untitled poems. *Open City* 3 (1995): 224–225.

Smith, Lee. "The Balsawood Man" (story). *Open City* 10 (2000): 203–206.

Smith, Molly. "untitled (underlie)" (drawings). *Open City* 21 (2005–2006): 41–48.

Smith, Peter Nolan. "Why I Miss Junkies" (story). *Open City* 13 (2001): 115–129.

Smith, Peter Nolan. "Better Lucky Than Good" (story). *Open City* 19 (2004): 65–70.

Smith, Rod. "Sandaled" (poem). *Open City* 14 (2001–2002): 145.

Snyder, Rick. "No Excuse," "Pop Poem '98" (poems). *Open City* 8 (1999): 151–152.

Smith, Dean. "Head Fake" (poem). *Open City* 1 (1992): 19–20.

Smith, Scott. "The Egg Man" (story). *Open City* 20 (2005): 1–67.

Solotaroff, Ivan. "Love Poem (On 53rd and 5th)" (poem). *Open City* 3 (1995): 228.

Solotaroff, Ivan. "Prince of Darkness" (story). *Open City* 6 (1998): 97–114.

Solotroff, Mark. "Fe·nes·tral Drawings" (drawings). *Open City* 18 (2003–2004): 213–218.

Southern, Nile. "Cargo of Blasted Mainframes" (story, drawings). *Open City* 1 (1992): 62–70.

Southern, Terry. "Twice on Top" (screenplay). *Open City* 2 (1993): 82–92.

Southern, Terry. "*C'est Toi Alors*: Scenario for Existing Props and French Cat" (screenplay). *Open City* 13 (2001): 41–43.

Space3. "Street Report EHV 003-2001" (prints). *Open City* 15 (2002): 159–164.

Spain, Chris. "The Least Wrong Thing" (story). *Open City* 26 (2008–2009): 33–52.

Specktor, Matthew. "A King in Mirrors" (story). *Open City* 26 (2008–2009): 59–72.

Staffel, Tim. "December 24, 1999–January 1, 2000" (story), trans. Elke Siegel and Paul Fleming. *Open City* 12 (2001): 95–118.

Stahl, Jerry. "Gordito" (story). *Open City* 22 (2006): 9–14.

Starkey, David. "Poem to Beer" (poem). *Open City* 12 (2001): 73–72.

Stefans, Brian Kim. "Two Pages from *The Screens*" (poem). *Open City* 14 (2001–2002): 163–165.

Stefans, Cindy. Photographs. *Open City* 6 (1998): 37–42.

Stefans, Cindy. Photographs. *Open City* 10 (2000): 115–124.

Stein, Lorin, trans., "Scenes from a Family Life" (story) by Véronique Ovaldé. *Open City* 21 (2005–2006): 141–152.

Stone, Nick. "Their Hearts Were Full of Spring" (photographs, text). *Open City* 10 (2000): 89–94.

Stone, Robert. "High Wire" (story). *Open City* 25 (2008): 1–38.

Strand, Mark. "Great Dog Poem No. 5" (poem). *Open City* 4 (1996): 145–146.

Stroffolino, Chris. "Nocturne," "Red Tape Sale" (poems). *Open City* 18 (2003–2004): 115–118.

Strouse, James C. "Goodbye, Blue Thunder" (story). *Open City* 19 (2004): 193–208.

Vapnyar, Lara. "Mistress" (story). *Open City* 15 (2002): 135–153.

Vapnyar, Lara. "There Are Jews in My House" (story). *Open City* 17 (2003): 243–273.

Vicente, Esteban. Paintings. *Open City* 3 (1995): 75–80.

Vicuña, Cecilia. "The Brilliance of Orifices," "Mother of Pearl," "The Anatomy of Paper" (poems), trans. Rosa Alcalá. *Open City* 14 (2001–2002): 151–154.

Walker, Wendy. "Sophie in the Catacombs" (story). *Open City* 19 (2004): 131–132.

Wallace, David Foster. "Nothing Happened" (story). *Open City* 5 (1997): 63–68.

Walls, Jack. "Hi-fi" (story). *Open City* 13 (2001): 237–252.

Walser, Alissa. "Given" (story), trans. Elizabeth Gaffney. *Open City* 8 (1999): 141–150.

Walsh, J. Patrick III. "It's time to go out on your own." (drawings). *Open City* 19 (2004): 35–40.

Wareck, Sarah Borden. "The Ambassador's Daughter" (story). *Open City* 25 (2008): 107–122.

Wareham, Dean. "Swedish Fish," "Orange Peel," "Weird and Woozy," "Romantica" (song lyrics). *Open City* 15 (2002): 197–200.

Webb, Charles H. "Vic" (poem). *Open City* 4 (1996): 134.

Weber, Paolina. Two Untitled Poems. *Open City* 3 (1995): 72–74.

Weber, Paolina. "Tape" (poems). *Open City* 9 (1999): 95–106.

Wefali, Amine. "Westchester Burning" (story). *Open City* 15 (2002): 59–75

Weiner, Cynthia. "Amends" (story). *Open City* 17 (2003): 71–89.

Welsh, Irvine. "Eurotrash" (story). *Open City* 3 (1995): 165–186.

Welsh, Irvine. "The Rosewell Incident" (story). *Open City* 5 (1997): 103–114.

Wenderoth, Joe. "Where God Is Glad" (essay). *Open City* 23 (2007): 209–216.

Wenderoth, Joe. "College," "Wedding Vow," "Against Zoning" (poems). *Open City* 23: (2007): 217–219.

Wenthe, William. "Against Witness" (poem). *Open City* 6 (1998): 115.

Wenthe, William. "Against Witness" (poem). *Open City* 12 (2001): 273.

Wenthe, William. "Shopping in Artesia" (poem). *Open City* 19 (2004): 63.

Wetzsteon, Rachel. "Largo," "Gusts" (poems). *Open City* 12 (2001): 285–286.

Weyland, Jocko. "Burrito" (story). *Open City* 6 (1998): 27–36.

Weyland, Jocko. "Swimmer Without a Cause" (story). *Open City* 10 (2000): 231–238.

Weyland, Jocko. "The Elk and the Skateboarder" (story). *Open City* 15 (2002): 169–187.

Weyland, Jocko. "Vietnam Is Number One" (story). *Open City* 22 (2006): 27–37.

Wheeler, Susan. "Barry Lyndon in Spring Lake, 1985" (poem). *Open City* 17 (2003): 115–116.

White, Edmund. "Harold Brodkey: The Great Pretender" (essay). *Open City* 27 (2009): 151–162.

Wier, Dara. "We Traveled by Night in a Ship Made of Ebony Splinters," "They Like to Say Light Is Your Shadow," "Something for You Because You Have Been Gone," "The Spirit of St. Louis" (poems). *Open City* 27 (2009): 47–50.